Open Souls

BECKY POURCHOT

Copyright © 2015 Becky Pourchot
All rights reserved.

No part of this book may be reproduced or transmitted in any form or by any means, electronic or mechanical, including photocopying, recording, or by any information storage and retrieval system, without written permission of the author, except for the inclusion of brief quotations in a review.

This is a work of fiction, names, characters, places, and incidents are fictitious, and any resemblance to actual persons, living or dead, business establishments, events, or locales is purely coincidental.

Published by Laughing Tiger Publications LLC
www.beckypourchot.com
April 2015

ISBN: 1508730121

ISBN-13: 978-1508730125

To Shawn,

who gets it.

Foreword

There are good books, and there are good stories. Sometimes, but not always, a good book contains a good story.

A good book is technically sound, well written, well edited, and will contain very little to anger the grammar-Nazis.

A good story is what keeps you turning the pages.

When you finish reading a good book, you close it and move on to the next one.

When you finish a good story, you wish there was more.

Similarly, there are good writers, and there are good story-tellers.

A good writer is technically proficient, follows the rules of grammar, dots all the *i's* and crosses all the *t's*.

A good story-teller will take you on a journey, introduce you to people and show you new places, all of which will become part of your reality.

Open Souls is a good book…but more importantly it's a good story.

First of all, it has a great *"what if"* concept.

The *what if*, in my opinion is the foundation upon which the story is built. Trying to build a good story on a weak *what if* is like trying to build a castle on a swamp.

What if there was a box which, when opened, caused those who opened it to lose their inhibitions, to abandon their fears, share their secrets, and pursue their innermost desires?

That's a great concept for a novel, one I wish I'd come up with, but it's only an idea – the next challenge is to craft a story worthy of such an idea, with characters strong enough to make the reader want to follow them on their journey.

Open Souls meets the challenge.

From the moment you begin reading you'll be pulled into the story, and when the story ends you won't want to be released from its grasp.

When I met Becky Pourchot she had two personal memoirs and a young-adult paranormal novella called *Food for a Hungry Ghost* to her credit. I enjoyed all of them, and it was obvious to me that she was a good writer as well as a very talented story-teller. She wrote two more installments in *The Hungry Ghost Series*, honing her skills with each one.

When she told me of her desire to venture into adult fiction I questioned her decision to abandon a genre in which she was clearly proficient.

Happily, my concerns were unfounded.

She has shown me, as she will soon show you, that her gift for telling a good story is not limited by genre.

In **Open Souls**, Becky puts you in St. Augustine and makes you feel as though you know Brad and Olivia personally.

She will also make you think twice before opening strange boxes…

Author, Tim Baker
www.timbaker.rocks

"Have I gone mad?"

"I'm afraid so, but let me tell you something, the best people usually are."

—Lewis Carroll, *Alice in Wonderland*

Prologue

Saint Augustine, Florida
1662

The smell of hot human bodies wafted towards Ana Martinez. She winced. This was to be the third hanging this summer in the Plaza de la Constitución. Whether the people on the stand deserved to die was irrelevant to the crowd around her. With the threat of pirate attacks, disease, and disaster always close at hand, there was nothing like a good lynching to distract their tired minds.

Ana fanned herself and stepped a few feet forward, giving herself space from a couple whose arguing had grown to an intolerable level. She didn't want to be there, not with that crowd: agitated, ornery, with death on their minds.

The only relief from the heat that day came from trees, their curly branches hanging overhead, but the shade did little to soothe Ana. It was the men, like the one today, whose wild, unabandoned, angry desire brought her here.

The crowd that day was so dense that it was hard for Ana to see the front stand—not that she wanted to see what was about to happen, but she needed to be prepared. She reached for the bag at her shoulder, checking to make sure its contents were still safe inside.

The executioner tightened the rope that hung from a branch above, testing its reliability.

Death had its own stench, as did hunger and desperation. This scent, she decided, was that of rabid fear, of humans holding on too tightly to the life that slipped past them all too easily. The executioner brought a man onto the platform and the crowd shifted, excitedly talking to one another.

The prisoner's hair was matted and oily, his clothes dank and urine stained. He squinted into the sun, looking out at the crowd below that surrounded him.

"Gonzalo Abano, you are hereby sentenced to death for theft and for the murder of your wife and children."

"Die, you swine!" someone called out from the audience, and a couple of men in the crowd jeered in agreement.

"Step up," the executioner commanded the man, whapping him on his back like a farmer to a belligerent cow. The man faltered a moment then stood on the stool as the crowd jeered and shouted.

A young woman holding a suckling baby at her breast called out, "Miserable shit!" spitting on the ground inches from Ana's feet

The crowd silenced as the executioner dropped the noose around the man's neck. It seemed to Ana that the birds in the park stopped their chirping simultaneously, as if they too knew what was coming.

Ana watched and waited, and even though she had been to ten of these hangings this year, her muscles tightened in nervous anticipation over what she was about to do.

The livid man spoke from his stool. "You ignorant fools! You are the sick ones. You will pay for your transgressions." And with his words he let out a laugh, dark and confident.

Then, with a grand gesture the executioner pushed a large wooden lever, causing a trap door to release. The man's body dropped and thrashed violently, resisting his impending death. After a few moments, when the fight became useless, the body stilled.

The crowd cheered, but for Ana the event wasn't over, yet. Acting quickly, she reached into her bag and pulled out a small wooden box etched with intricate baroque vines and lettering. Watching the swinging body, she held the box tight in her hands.

Within a few moments it happened. A thin ribbon of smoke emerged from the corpse, snaking its way around its former body as if to verify its hollow remains were real.

The crowd was oblivious, but Ana saw it and knew well. Never having grown accustomed to the demon-like presence of a soul such as this man's, her heart raced, and the being seemed to grow in size, becoming more human in shape as it swooped around its former body then ventured out over the crowd, beneath the oaks, the echoing, angry laughter of the dead man reverberating through the trees.

Ana opened the box and began speaking quietly to herself, "Non plus chaos, non plus chaos, non plus chaos," and she watched with focus as the soul, against its own wild will, was pulled towards the box.

The magnetism between the small magic box and the shadow creature was strong, forcing Ana to hold on tight, her muscles shaking as she kept the box in place.

"Non plus chaos, non plus chaos," she continued to mutter, and the darkened creature, shrinking with its approach, filled the box with its black emptiness. When the last strands of its being made their way in, Ana closed the box and latched it tight with a clasp. As the unknowing crowd dispersed, returning to their work-laden lives, she cupped her hands over the box, brought it close to her heart, and exhaled.

With the plaza now cleared, Ana opened her hands and let the delicately carved box rest in her palms, the wood now warm from the magic she had conjured. With her finger she traced three scripted words on the lid and whispered again in Latin: "No more chaos." She then slipped the box into her bag and headed north.

As she walked the half mile to her one-room cottage on Saint George Street, she noticed a white and black sea bird—an osprey, flying overhead.

"A good omen," she thought, and she opened the crooked wooden door to her cottage and entered.

The cottage walls were lined with shelves, most of them containing corked ceramic jars labeled with the names of medicinal herbs and concoctions, but one shelf was different. Lined with care were more than thirty small, wooden boxes, just like the one Ana held in her bag. Each one was adorned with its own version of the carving—vines, flowers, trees, and birds—and each held the same Latin phrase Ana had used to bind the box.

She pulled the prison-like box from her bag. "To never be opened again," she whispered in Spanish as she gently placed it in an empty space beside its sister boxes.

That night, Ana found it hard to sleep. Nightmares of the collected souls being set free into the world haunted her. As she lay there, heart racing, staring at the timbers of her ceiling, she heard a scream coming from a nearby home. The sounds of men yelling in English surrounded the cottage. Ana sat up in bed and pulled the curtain to one side. The light from lanterns swayed, and she could make out a tall man holding her neighbor against the point of his sword as another man torched the nearby mill.

She climbed out of bed, grabbed a kitchen knife from the hearth and quickly wrapped her hands around it as she waited in the corner.

Within moments the door was pushed open by a disheveled man with a sword in one hand, a lantern in the other. Illuminated from below, his soot-marked, sallow skin seemed goblin-like as the tall shadows he cast from the light fluctuated in a foreboding dance.

Ana's mother had survived the first pirate attack on Saint Augustine, and Ana was hell bent to do the same. Without hesitation, she lunged at him with the knife. He dodged it to one side and grabbed her.

The pirate chuckled, pulling the knife from her hand. Ana tried to wriggle away, but he had twice her strength. She gritted her teeth and growled. Holding her thrashing body at bay, the pirate scanned the room for treasures.

He spoke in English. "So, we have a little witch girl." He laughed.

Ana understood the English word "witch" and in a panic resisted with all her strength. He looked down at her with a lustful eye.

"Satan's mistress, eh?" he said as he pulled her in and wrapped his arm around her waist. The smell of the filthy sailor engulfed her.

"You know what we do with pagan tramps?" he asked, raising his sword, but before he acted he paused as he noticed the wall of boxes.

"What's this?" he asked, his eyes wide.

He put down his sword and released Ana by shoving her to the floor. As she clambered for the free weapon, he nonchalantly pushed her away with a boot into her face.

Taking a box from the shelf, he turned it around in his hands, brought it to his ear, and shook it.

"No, no, no!" she said, crying.

He looked at her and snickered then tossed the box into a leather bag.

He grabbed another. Ana rose to her feet with what little strength she had and lunged for it. She tugged at his arm and shouted in Spanish, "These must never be opened!"

"Get off me, you beast," he said, and then as if discarding a rat that had entered his home, he pulled a knife from his waist and stabbed it deep into her stomach.

She felt the piercing pain radiate outward, and the taste of blood crept up her throat. She began to cough, each heaving movement of her belly building the tide of pain. She grasped at the knife and tried to pull it out.

The man leaned down close to her, and she begged him to remove the knife. Laughing, he tore it from her belly then casually wiped the blood from the blade on his pants.

"Witch whore," he spat at her in English.

Ana watched in terror as he began tossing the boxes into the bag with a wild, hungry grin.

She tried calling out but there was no air left to speak. Helplessly, she watched as he threw the last wooden box into his sack and the world became dark.

Chapter 1

Saint Augustine, Florida

Present Day

Brad watched as Courtney shook her hips and hummed along to the radio, sweeping the floor with the enthusiasm of a stripper with a pole. Her ass was magnificent. Truly a work of art. And every time she shook it, it killed Brad just a little bit inside.

She was of legal age—nineteen, which was, technically, fair game—but she was his employee and the granddaughter of his best friend, Dog. He glanced over at her rear again and felt that recurring ache.

Brad snapped himself out of his ass-induced trance by addressing his other employee. "Hey, Buzz, tell that lady of yours to stop shaking her rump around. We're trying to concentrate," he said, dipping a tattoo needle into a vial of ink.

Courtney looked back at Brad with a sly smile and gave her butt a nice shake. She knew as well as any of them that her backside had the power to make men melt.

Off limits, Brad thought to himself, knowing full well that it would not be good to do his best buddy's granddaughter.

Darren, Brad's current customer, winced a little when the needles hit the soft fleshy spot on his arm.

"You okay, buddy?" Brad asked him, pausing for a moment.

"Fine. Keep going," his client answered through his teeth.

Then, trying to sound collected, Darren added, "Courtney, why don't you come over here and give me a little of that tail wagging . . . distract me from Brad's heavy hand." Darren was a regular, currently entrusting Brad to do an entire right-arm sleeve.

Brad continued etching freehand on his customer's flesh, wondering to himself whether hiring Courtney on as a body piercer was going to be a help to the business or just be a complete distraction for everyone.

With wrinkles setting in around his forehead and his mouth, grey streaks mixing with the brown in his hair, Brad was looking his age. He may have no longer been the same robust man he was thirty years back, but his playful, tough-guy allure always outshined his age. Courtney made her way over to Brad's booth, her hips still shaking with each pass of the broom.

"Damn, man, stop being such a slut," Buzz called to her across the studio. Buzz had been apprenticing under Brad for three months and dating Courtney for about that time as well. The kid was cocky and did shoddy work.

"Aww, I'm just playin' with him," Courtney said, letting her fingers playfully caress Brad's neck.

Brad felt a wave of warmth run up his spine as her hands caressed his shoulders. Fuck, this girl was driving him mad.

"Hey, hey, hey—watch it, little lady," Dog called from across the room, wagging his finger at his granddaughter. "No touching the doctor during surgery."

Courtney looked at her grandpa and frowned when she noticed the cream-filled éclair in his hand.

"Another donut, Gramps? Really? Don't diabetics get their feet cut off for eating too many sweets?"

Buzz snickered, "Yeah. Pretty soon we'll be calling you Limpy . . . Grandpa *Limpy.*"

Nobody laughed but Buzz.

He knew he crossed the line, but he snickered to himself anyway. Brad muttered something about Buzz being a royal ass.

Courtney may have been able to call Dog out on his health, but that was it. Not even Brad, his best friend, had the freedom to do so. Dog was the oldest of Brad's employees, twelve years Brad's senior, and though Dog wasn't boss, he garnered a certain level of respect around the shop. Everyone else knew where the line was. Apparently Buzz did, too; he just didn't care.

Ignoring Buzz's stupid remark Dog walked his lanky, six-foot-four body over to Brad, who was still working on Darren's arm. Courtney was straddling a chair backwards, watching Brad, as well.

"One donut ain't gonna kill me, hon," Dog said. "I can take care of myself just fine. Now, why don't you go shake that butt of yours somewhere else?"

Courtney stood up and walked off.

Dog scanned Brad's handiwork and nodded. "Mmm hmm. Nice job as always, my friend," he said, stroking his long white beard.

Dog had been tattooing since the Seventies, when customers just picked their tats off of the flash rack. "None of the fancy schmancy custom crap," he'd always say, but regardless he appreciated his buddy's artful take on tattooing.

Brad had been Dog's protégé thirty years back, like Buzz was to Brad now. Within a year of Brad's apprenticeship, Brad was tattooing better than Dog was. While Dog was a craftsman, a paint-by-numbers sort of guy, Brad was an artist, channeling his care and energy into every piece he created.

Brad had eventually built himself a good reputation in Saint John's County and opened Phoenix Tattoo—his own shop on Saint George Street. Dog had stood by his side every step of his journey. When the shop opened eight years ago, he joined him.

"Brad, did you need me to dust the cabinets tonight?" Courtney asked, now by the cash register, a spray bottle in hand.

"Nah, that's okay. Just wipe down the piercings cabinet and call it a day."

Brad rubbed the excess ink off his customer's arm and admired his handiwork.

"You're good to go, Darren. Come back in a week and I'll finish up on the raven," Brad said, holding up a mirror. Darren gave his reflection a big smile.

"This is fantastic as always, dude. Thanks," he said, giving Brad a strong handshake.

"Now, remember: Keep it clean and lubed up . . . you know the drill."

As he spoke, Brad's phone chirped. He pulled it out of his pocket and read the text from a name not listed in his phone.

The message read:

"Great time last night. When can I see you again?"

Brad had to think for a second before remembering who it was. Then it came to him. Monica was a girl he had picked up at Finn's Bar and banged one night under the stairway. He put the phone back in his pocket and decided not to text her back.

He offered Darren his weathered hand for support.

"Get up slowly, bud. You've been sitting here a long time."

Darren took his hand, carefully rose up, and walked to the front counter, where Courtney rang him up.

Dog, who had spent the day waiting for walk-ins, glanced at the clock. Never as many people just showed up for impromptu tattoos as they used to, but Dog was getting old and no longer particularly cared how busy he was. Bike Week and Biketoberfest, when the motorcycles came to town, were enough to supply him with money for beer and weed. His wife, Suzanne, who refused to retire, was making pretty good money at the DMV. Luckily Dog's growing doctor bills were mostly covered by vet benefits.

"I'm done for the day, bud," Dog said, returning a set of inks to the cabinet and slipping his wallet and keys into his pocket.

"All right. I'll see ya tomorrow," Brad said, standing to give his buddy a hearty pat on the back.

"Suze and I are headed down to White Eagle tomorrow night. Some chick is playing—Jasmine Kane—Suze says she's good. You want to join us? I can't guarantee you'll get laid, but who knows?"

"Hmm. I'd be up for that . . . though I'm telling you, I'm done with women for a while. Too demanding. No more."

Dog just laughed. "Yeah, good luck with that," he said.

Brad nodded with a smile. "Yeah, thanks, friend."

"Bye, Gramps!" Courtney called across the studio.

"Bye, sugar plum," Dog said as he stepped out the door.

Buzz was still at a light-box working on the same drawing he had been at most of the day. Eraser shavings were spread around his space.

"Bye, honey bunny sweetie," he tittered, mimicking Dog's gravelly, old-man voice.

Brad looked over and glared at him. "Hey, you cocky shit, why don't you stop with that drawing? I need you to stay after and do a check of the stock room. I'm placing an order tomorrow."

"Uh, okay," Buzz said, putting down his pencil.

Buzz headed towards the back of the store where Courtney, finished with her jobs, had hiked herself up onto the glass countertop and was checking her eye makeup in a mirror. She opened her knees towards Buzz as he approached with an eager smile.

"Mmm hmm, baby. I'll give it to you right here. Uh, uh," he said, stepping between her legs and thrusting his hips.

Courtney giggled and opened her legs wider.

Brad looked up. "Hey, guys. Really? Court, get down. You're going to break the glass."

Buzz backed away from his girlfriend and snickered, "You hear that? The old man thinks you've got a fat ass, babe."

"Sorry, Brad," she said, sliding herself down, looking hurt. "Do you think my ass is big, Buzz?" she asked as she twisted around, trying to see her bottom.

"Yes. Duh. It's big. Like, ginormous big."

"But, big in a good way, right?" she looked to Brad, hoping for some support.

"I'm staying out of this," he said, holding his hands up defensively.

Buzz snickered and headed to the back room. Holding a clipboard, he began taking notes. Courtney joined him.

"You still think I'm hot, right?" she asked, her voice trailing from the back room.

"Yes. Look, you've got a fat ass. Deal with it. Leave me alone so I can get this done."

Rejected, Courtney returned to the front room where she perched herself on a stool like a disciplined circus poodle. Buzz finished with his notes then slapped the clipboard on the glass counter. He walked up to Brad. "I'm done, man. Can I go now?"

Brad noticed the smell of metabolized alcohol wafting his way and wondered if Buzz had been drinking all day. Not wanting a confrontation, Brad let it go.

"Yeah, you can go," he answered.

"You still giving me a ride?" Courtney asked Buzz cautiously.

"Yeah. Whatever," Buzz said

"Can we swing by my mom's? I need to pick up my laundry I left there."

"Why the fuck do we always have to stop at your mom's after work? You know I can't stand that bitch."

Courtney looked as if she had just been slapped in the face. Brad fumed, but he refrained from saying anything and just watched quietly out of the corner of his eye as he cleaned up his station.

"It'll just be a second. You can stay in the car. I need my clothes."

"You know what? Fuck your laundry. Go get it on your own time. I'm sick of this shit." And with that he stormed out of the shop and slammed the door behind him. The sound of his beat-up Chevy driving away vibrated the shop windows.

Courtney stood alone in the center of the store, her hands hanging at her sides like she was a piece of limp seaweed washed up on shore. Brad faked working on a drawing just to avoid being sucked into her drama.

"Buzz gets like this sometimes," she said softly. "It'll be all right. He'll come around," she said, convincing herself.

Brad stayed at his booth and watched from a distance as Courtney's eyes turned into liquefied pools. He knew what was coming, and he wasn't looking forward to it.

The girl now stood as an isolated island in the brightness of the room. Her shoulders heaving in small, restrained sobs, her face was now ugly and contorted in defeat.

Brad didn't want to leave his seat. He hated crying just about as much as he hated drunken assholes like Buzz. Yet the sobbing continued and he knew as a man, as her boss, as her grandpa's best friend that he had to help. He stood up slowly and walked over to her, put a tentative arm around her back and patted a little too strongly. She blinked her eyes in surprise at his poor attempt at tenderness.

"Buzz is a jerk. You know that," Brad said.

She gave him a concerned look. "You're not going to fire him, are you?"

Courtney was naïve to think that Brad would put up with Buzz's antics. There was no place for drinking or verbal abuse in his shop. That kind of behavior might have been tolerated at other places in town, but Brad was not the combative biker guy that his image portrayed. In fact, he absolutely loathed conflict. His temper only came out when he was pushed past his limit, which was almost never. Calm and centered was the way he preferred to be.

Brad looked her straight in the eyes.

"I'll be honest with you, Courtney; I think this was the last straw for him."

Courtney began crying again, this time in loud sobs. "It's my fault, isn't it?"

Brad's body constricted a little tighter with each of her sobs and for one moment he actually looked towards the door with a plan to escape, but instead he patted her again.

"Look. It'll be okay. Buzz is just starting out. He'll find other work," he said, but his words had no effect. She just kept crying.

He put his hand on her arm and looked at her. She blinked, as her watery eyes focused on his bristly chin.

"You don't need him, anyway. The guy is a creep. Really. You can do better."

She looked at him with her soft eyes. "You really think so?"

"Yeah, I know so. I mean, a hot girl like you could have anyone."

She blinked a couple more times, and her lips softened.

"How about you?" she asked, relaxing her body ever so slightly.

She brought herself to him and he felt her melt into his body. She would be a marvelous lay, he knew, but he kept thinking of Dog and how pissed he would be.

"Hey Courtney, this is not what I meant. I mean, you were like in kindergarten when I was moving on to my second wife." He laughed awkwardly, but she kept looking at him, gently curving her round lips into a soft frown.

New tears formed in her eyes, and she said, "I'm so stupid. I'm sorry. I'm just feeling really vulnerable right now."

"Yeah, no shit," Brad said with a nervous snicker. "Look, I just don't want to do something you and I will regret."

She gave him a look of innocent rejection, and his eye fell onto her slight valley of cleavage. To contain himself, he began a little mantra: *I'm her boss. I'm her boss. I'm her boss.* But, somehow, that just seemed to make him more aroused.

Courtney wiped her eyes then took Brad's hand, "*I* won't regret it," she said. Then, seeming a lot less sad, she took his hand and placed it on her left breast.

"How about we just don't go all the way . . . just a little touching," she said softly, her hand wandering to his cock. "There's nothing wrong with that."

Brad's knees just about buckled. His mantra of self-control fell into the distance as he found himself weak to his own will.

He lowered her into one of the tattoo chairs and looked down at her, her eyes still puffy from crying, a smudge of mascara running down her cheek.

"Give it to me," she said, and in that moment, like he'd done way too many times before, he let go of any semblance of responsibility and surrendered to the heat.

Chapter 2

All of the cupcakes were burnt—one hundred and eight to be exact. Olivia opened the front door to the bakery, releasing the smoke-filled air onto Saint George Street. Passing tourists on the pedestrians-only street wrinkled their noses as the smell of acrid, black sugar billowed past.

She grabbed the phone and hit speed dial.

"Mandie, the cupcakes for the Schwarz bar mitzvah are ruined."

"Aw, fucking shit!" The woman said on the other line, a hint of Southern twang wrapped into her obscenities. "What happened?"

"You didn't set the timer." Olivia pressed the phone between her ear and shoulder as she removed the desiccated remains from the oven. "I didn't know you put them in. You left so fast," Olivia said, gritting her teeth.

On the line she could hear a man's voice in the background.

Mandie's voice became muffled. "Dude. I'm on the phone," she said to someone in the room with her.

"Just pass it over. Give me a hit," the man in the background answered. Olivia recognized the other voice as belonging to Tank, Mandie's off- and on-again boyfriend.

Mandie returned to the phone, her voice tight now, apparently holding smoke in her lungs.

"Well, fuck, man. No cupcakes? You're going to have to make more."

Olivia imagined her friend sitting in bed beside her boyfriend, Tank, in their underwear, passing a joint between them.

Olivia had tried pot several times with an old boyfriend, during her days at Flagler College, but the marijuana had just made things really weird—and had made her hungry. Neither of which she particularly appreciated.

"You cool with this?" Mandie asked.

"Yeah, no problem," Olivia said, but it wasn't with her regular enthusiasm.

"You're awesome. I'll be back in—I promise," she said her voice tightening again as she took another hit.

Olivia had met Mandie at Flagler College in their Renaissance Art History class. Mandie had asked Olivia to work with her on a collaborative project. She had been behind on the readings, so Olivia, who looked like she was on top of things, seemed like an obvious choice.

Olivia, who had only a scattering of friends, had been excited and honored that her classmate who dressed like June Clever's saucy stepsister wanted to be her partner.

It turned out that they were a great team. Olivia used her love of detail, while Mandie offered her artistic flair and sense of humor to keep them both afloat. They had ended up acing the project.

The front door jingled. Olivia quickly washed her hands and straightened her apron. A young girl and her mom stood at the counter. The child's eyes were wide with excitement.

"Hi! Welcome to Eat it Too," Olivia said, tucking her mousy brown hair behind her ears.

"This place is so fun," the mom said, looking around. "We've vacationed in Saint Augustine for years, but I never even knew this was here," she added, turning to look at a mural that was hot glued with sea shells, beads, and the occasional Barbie doll head.

A mutual friend of Mandie's and Olivia's once joked that the shop looked like it had been sieged by Chinese trinkets, with every crevice covered in plastic skeletons, rubber zombies, and other odds and ends all interspersed with Mardi Gras beads and sparkling craft-shop jewels. Being in Saint Augustine, one of the nation's most haunted cities, this went over quite well with the tourists. Olivia thought, in spite of the décor's odd content, the effect was quite lovely, and their customers agreed.

"Kaylee, isn't this place so clever?" the mom asked.

The girl, with a skull bow in her hair, glanced over at a row of plastic doll limbs embedded in the wall with a huge grin on her face then returned her eyes to the pastry case.

"My business partner did all these murals herself. She is an artist and a baker," Olivia said.

"My goodness. Such talent in this town," the mom said, clucking her tongue. She turned to her daughter. "So, Kaylee, what looks good to you?"

"I can't decide," she answered.

The mom leaned down to get a closer look at the case.

"Ooh, Satan's Seduction looks good…hmm, but so does Caramel Carnage." She then looked to Olivia. "Does the Severed Finger really have homemade raspberry preserves inside?"

"Yes, both the Severed Finger and the Internal Hemorrhage have jam made from organic local berries. We make it all here on site," Olivia said reflexively.

"Well, we certainly need to pick up those for Dad and Joe," the mom said, looking down at her daughter.

The bakery phone rang and Olivia excused herself.

"Hello? Eat it Too, where you can have your cupcake and eat it, too. This is Olivia speaking," she said.

"Hi, this is Claudia Schwarz. I was wondering if I could come by early and pick up the cupcakes for my grandson's bar mitzvah," the woman said with a heavy New York accent.

"Oh . . . yes. I am sorry. They aren't quite ready yet. Could you come by at five?"

"Five is not an option. The girl I talked to earlier said they'd be ready by two."

"Again, I'm so sorry. I can have them by three. How's that?"

Three o'clock would be a daunting task for Olivia, but it was better than dealing with the wrath of a furious Bar Mitzvah Grandmother.

"I suppose," the woman said, clearly miffed.

"Again, I apologize, ma'am. We'll see you soon."

Olivia hung up the phone. The girl and her mom were now looking upward, discussing the ceiling fan that had silver skulls glittered onto its blades.

"So very clever," the mom kept saying.

Olivia knew after having the shop for five years that when women clucked their tongues and said "clever" or "fascinating" they were hiding the fact that they were actually a tad creeped out by the whole thing. Nevertheless, kids, bikers, artist types, and tourists always loved it. Soccer moms, like this woman, just endured it to keep their children happy.

Olivia finished with her customers, picked up the phone, and dialed Mandie again.

"Mandie, the Schwarz lady called again. I told her we'd have the cupcakes by three."

"What!? You can't do it by then." A small dog began barking in the background.

"Newton, shut up!" Mandie yelled into the receiver. Her parrot joined in with the clamor.

"I know it's going to be tight. I'm sorry," Olivia said masking her anger. "You need to come in."

"Crap," Mandie grumbled.

The barking dog continued. "Fuck, Newton! Shut up, guys! All right. I'll be there in twenty minutes. Start the buttercream before I get there," she said and hung up.

Six years back, Mandie had approached Olivia with a "crazy-ass idea." Mandie had told her she was thinking of quitting school and starting a full-time cupcake business, but she couldn't do it alone. She needed Olivia with her minor in business management and that rigid sense of order that Mandie lacked.

With a lot of prodding, Olivia had agreed and dropped out as well, with the resolution that she would finish her last two semesters in a few years when the business was established. As enticing as co-owning a shop was to Olivia initially, it was now five years into the business and she had not yet returned to school, and Mandie's carefree attitude was becoming Olivia's burden.

About an hour later, Mandie showed up at the bakery looking fabulous. Her black hair up in tight pin curl, she wore a black button-up rockabilly dress with a poofy crinoline underneath. She walked over, her red heels clicking across the floor. She gave Olivia a big hug.

"Girl, you are a life saver. You're, like, amazing."

As Mandie talked, Olivia watched her bright red lips. She gave her a half smile, resisting the resentment that bubbled inside of her.

"Oh, my gosh, you have to see our new uniforms," Mandie said, more relaxed than she should be for the pressing moment. She pulled out a frilled, lacy black and white apron that looked more like a sex shop's French maid costume than bakery attire.

"I'm thinking we can wear these every day. . . you know, with some fishnets and heels. We can sex the whole place up a little."

Putting aside her anger, Olivia wiped her hands on a towel and reached for the apron.

"We can be the saucy bakers of Saint Augustine," Mandie said, slipping it over her own head. She tied the ribbon tight around the waist, revealing her curvy hips and generous chest.

As ridiculous as the aprons were, Mandie looked good. She always looked good. Men came into the store just to talk to her. She had this way of looking at them, bringing one shoulder forward in an almost unperceivable gesture—just enough to suggest vulnerability and sexual power at the same time.

"Put it on, Livia! I want to see," Mandie said, handing Olivia a matching one.

Olivia pulled the apron over her head and tied the waist. Mandie nodded, like a man pleased with a dancer at a strip club.

"Mmm . . . yeah, hot mama. You've got it going on, babe."

Olivia's attempt at a smile came out more like a frown one might see on an old tortoise.

"Honey, seriously, I don't know why you dress yourself in that J. Crew crap. You've got the body, why hide it? Seriously, you're smoking. I mean, hell, I'd do you," Mandie said with a long grin.

Olivia glanced at her friend. Mandie was a monument of organized chaos, always offering a relaxed laugh, a playful joke, in spite of everything around being on the verge of exploding. She was enticing, appealing. People loved her. Olivia was hopelessly bound to this woman. Olivia dropped two pounds of butter into an industrial mixer and watched it disperse with the spinning blades.

Mandie continued, "I'm just saying, girl. You've got the goods, flaunt 'em." She walked over to the flour-dusted iPod dock and turned up the volume until the Rolling Stones were so loud that casual conversation was impossible. For that, Olivia was grateful. Mandie's monthly lectures about Olivia's need for sexual liberation were getting old. She knew she was uptight, but no advice from Mandie was going to loosen her up; in fact, it just made things worse.

Mic Jagger wailed,

I can't get no...
Sat-is-faction.

... and Olivia heard a muffled call from the front room.

"Hellooo?"

Olivia turned the music down and peeked out.

A short woman wearing a bright hibiscus-patterned blouse was standing in the front, looking annoyed.

"Well, it's about time. I've been here for ten minutes."

"I'm so sorry," Olivia said wiping her hands on her apron.

"I'm Ruth Schwarz, picking up the chocolate ganache cupcakes for the bar mitzvah."

Olivia looked at the clock. It was only two fifteen.

"They're not ready, yet. I think we agreed on three o'clock, right?"

"This is ridiculous. My grandson insisted I order cupcakes here even though I knew it was a bad idea. I agreed because you girls have an excellent reputation, but now you're telling me I can't have them when I want them? Meanwhile, you're just playing around back there like you're at the Whisky a Go Go. Listen, honey, your party is over. I need my cupcakes."

Mandie stepped out from the kitchen.

"Hi, can I help you?"

Mrs. Schwarz eyed her up and down, her gaze fixing upon the naked devil-lady tattoo resting on her right breast.

"Yes, I'd like to speak to the manager. I'm Claudia Schwarz. I'm here for my cupcakes, but this girl seems to think they aren't ready."

Mandie gave Mrs. Schwarz a big lipstick grin.

"Oh yes, Ruth. We talked on the phone last week. I remember. Nothing bloody or gory, just small sugar skulls, right?" Mandie's eyes twinkled just so. "You asked to keep it tasteful for your *son* Josh's, bar mitzvah, right?

Mrs. Schwarz's posture softened.

"Grandson, actually," she smiled.

"Are you kidding? I can't believe you're a grandmother!"

The woman's face blossomed pink.

Mandie had her right where she wanted her. "But, hey, listen," she said. "I am so sorry. We've been having problems with our ovens and unfortunately your cupcakes have been delayed. But, you know what? We'll have them in your hands by two fifty-five. And, to show you how greatly sorry I am, I'd like to offer you a complimentary dozen of our double chocolate Hissing Cockroach cupcakes. Josh will love them!"

Olivia, taking her cue, headed for the case and filled a box with the cupcakes topped with rubber bugs. The grandmother was clearly pleased with herself, believing she earned free cupcakes through her combativeness.

The two women returned to the back room and scrambled to get the baking done. At three o'clock, Mrs. Schwarz returned and didn't even bat an eyelash that she had to wait fifteen minutes for the girls to finish up. She left the bakery pleased as a petunia.

After closing that evening, Olivia walked the short distance home, past the stores on narrow Saint George Street and past the Plaza de la Constitución. Ancient oaks hung heavy with Spanish moss above her head as she followed the trail along the park.

An older couple sat on a bench with a map of the area, debating whether to foot it to the Old Jail or grab the trolley. After nine years in Saint Augustine, all tourists looked the same to Olivia. This couple, she guessed, was from somewhere way north—Massachusetts, maybe. Clearly, neither of them had anticipated how ungodly hot Florida was in the summer as they sweated in their long pants and button-up shirts.

Olivia was exhausted from dealing with people all day, but she also felt a duty to help out when she could. Pulling back that tight smile that had become a rehearsed gesture in her career in customer service, she said, "Hey. Um. I recommend you take the trolley to the Old Jail. It's only about a fifteen-minute walk, but it's pretty hot today."

"Oh! Thank you, miss. We really appreciate it," said the man, folding up the map and dabbing his brow with a handkerchief. Olivia started stepping away, but the man called after her.

"So, you're from around here, I take it?"

"Yes," Olivia said.

"We're thinking about relocating. You happy here?" he asked, his mouth moving behind a silver mustache.

"Yeah," she said, shrugging her shoulders.

"So, not so much?" the man asked, reading her ambivalence.

"No, it's fine. It's as good a place as any to live, I suppose," she said. Wanting to avoid more conversation, she aimed her body again in the direction of home.

The rest of the way back she pondered the man's question. Was she happy here? No one had ever asked her that.

She should be happy, right? She owned a thriving business, had a stable boyfriend, lived in a town full of history, had great cultural events all within biking distance. But, was she happy? She didn't know. Truthfully, she wasn't sure what, if a*nything,* made her happy. She shrugged the thought away.

Chapter 3

Olivia lived near the center of town not far from King Street in a small Cracker-style house with a big old porch that slouched down in the front toward the sidewalk. Her rental consisted of the entire second floor. She climbed the indoor stairs to her flat, hung her bag on a hook, picked up her phone, and dialed her boyfriend, Andrew.

By Olivia's account, her relationship with Andrew was going "just fine." He was easy to be with and didn't expect much from her. He let her pick most of the movies they'd watch, what restaurants they'd go to, who they'd hang out with. He pretty much did as she requested, and that was okay by Olivia. However, she had once told Mandie that her feelings for Andrew were a lot like her feelings towards tapioca pudding or easy-listening music—neutral, without passion.

Andrew answered Olivia's call on the first ring. "Hello, my love!"

"Do you want to finish up season two of *Buffy the Vampire Slayer* tonight?" she asked.

"Of course!"

"I'll see you in a few, then?" she asked.

"Can't wait," he said.

Andrew had thin hands and long toes that seemed to hang over his sandals when he walked. He was an intense guy—at least when it came to talking about postmodern literature, his favorite subject to teach at the college. Every once in a while when he got excited talking about *Don Quixote*, he'd flick his wrists like a woman as he spoke. He wasn't gay, but the more Olivia knew him, the more his feminine traits appeared. She told herself it was his gentlemanly nature, but she was never convinced.

Olivia's cat, Lucy, rubbed up and down on her leg as Olivia walked about the apartment, tidying up her already orderly place. As she set her well-worn *Field Guide to Shore Birds* prominently on top of a stack of magazines, she noticed the French maid apron had fallen out of her bag. She lifted it and looked at it, then held it up to her body, sucked in her imaginary gut, and glanced at her reflection in the antique mirror on the other side of the room. She jutted out her chest, puckered her lips a bit, and raised her eyebrows. She looked ridiculous.

Olivia quickly stuffed the apron back into the bag as she heard the telltale squeak of approaching steps on the wooden stairs followed by a rapid knock on the door. A dozen pink roses were pushed towards her face when she opened it.

"For you, m'lady," Andrew said. She took them, breathed in the grocery store scent, and forced a smile.

"What are these for?" she asked.

"Our eight-month anniversary. Don't you remember? Our first date was a week before Christmas."

Olivia did the math in her head. "Yeah. Right . . . I'm sorry, I don't have anything for you."

"No worries. Your presence is the best present." He raised his eyebrows amused at his own play on words, then his face lit up. "Oh, I almost forgot!"

He handed her a small black cardboard box with a stock photo of a man and woman in a silhouetted embrace.

She looked at it blankly.

"His and her *lubricants*!" he said, excited.

"Really?" she asked.

"Well, yeah," he said bringing his face in close to hers and raising an eyebrow.

"But what about *Buffy*?" she asked.

He moved in and whispered, "She can wait."

He placed his lips on hers gently. While keeping her body protected and stiff, she reciprocated. She didn't know why this was always so difficult for her. She wasn't in the mood, she rarely was, but she did have sympathy for his "needs." It had been awhile since they had done it.

The French maid apron and Mandie's insistence on sexing her life up came to mind. Maybe she just needed the right finessing.

"Hold on," she said, breaking away from him. She grabbed her bag and slipped into her room. A few minutes later she stepped out, wearing nothing but the apron, the sides of her breasts peeking out around the edges.

"Hmm, yeah," Andrew grinned like a twelve-year-old boy opening his first *Playboy*. He plopped himself down on the couch. His legs were spread wide, welcoming her approach as he unzipped his shorts.

"I'm a dirty boy, miss maid. I think I need you to clean me *all over*."

She brought herself to the couch and he wrapped his arms around her as she straddled him. She could feel his hardness firmly pressed against her.

I want this, she told herself, but her body, taciturn and stiff, disagreed.

"Come on. Play along, Liv. You're the naughty French maid coming to my home to clean me up. I'm a very dirty boy."

"I . . ." she stammered as she tried to pull up some smart, sexy line for him, but nothing came to her. In fact, all she wanted to do was run to her bedroom and put on her flannel pajamas.

"Oh, baby. You are so hot," he said into her ear, gyrating his hips slowly. She felt a faint tinge of arousal rise in her, but it died as quickly as it had come. The hot scent of hummus and pickles on his breath was too much to bear. She pulled back.

"What? Sweetie?"

She shook her head, pulled herself off of him, and went to the kitchen, covering her face.

He followed after her.

She was now at the sink, staring at the hanging prism that spun in the window in front of her. Andrew wrapped his arm around her and rubbed her shoulders.

"You know this is okay . . . if you're not in the mood, I'm okay with that. I just want to do what makes you happy."

"I know," she said. "I'm sorry. Really."

"It's okay, hon. I like you just the way you are."

Olivia wiped her eyes. Offering him a concession she said, "Do you want to stay the night, anyway?"

"Of course," he said.

The next morning at six fifteen, Olivia rolled out of bed, her t-shirt wrinkled, her dark hair stuck to the side of her head. She entered the kitchen. Andrew stood in his tighty whiteys at the stove, making eggs Benedict. He was singing the same Barry White tune he always sang while making breakfast in her home.

Olivia looked at him with guilt in her eyes.

"What's that look?" Andrew asked.

"Just happy, I suppose."

He grinned wide. "Me, too."

Andrew gave her a kiss on the cheek then handed her a plate brimming with the eggs Benedict, hash browns, and fresh strawberries.

Olivia took her knife and divided her food into piles, setting boundaries that defined which foods and how much of each she would allow herself to enjoy. This was a ritual she started way back in high school to control her weight, even though it had never been an issue. Somewhere deep inside she believed that this little ritual, this act of division, kept her life from unraveling.

Andrew looked at her plate and smiled. "It's okay to eat the whole thing, you know?"

"I know," she said a little defensively. She finished eating her portion and wrapped the remaining half for later.

"You don't need to diet for me. You're beautiful just the way you are."

"I suppose," she shrugged.

"You have time for a quickie?" he asked with playful lust in his eye.

She glanced at the kitchen clock and shook her head. "I'm afraid not."

She went to the bedroom to get dressed. He followed her and talked all the while about his PhD thesis. Andrew had been her professor in English 101, which was how they had met. The class was a requirement for her double major, but her interest in literary theory stopped there. When they began dating, he enjoyed talking finance management with her, a topic she loved, but now it was all about Miguel de Cervantes Saavedra, a long-dead author, who Olivia was pretty sure Andrew had some sort of man crush on.

He watched closely as she slipped on her jeans and buttoned up her blouse. She moved to the bathroom and he followed, now watching as she brushed her teeth.

"I love you, you know," he said to the Olivia in the mirror.

No man, other than her dad, had said these words to her, but rather than making her feel comforted and uplifted, Andrew's comment made her feel hollow, reminding her of the gaping distance she felt between herself and him. She was alone, and his words just reinforced it.

Even at the age of twenty-seven, love was a difficult concept for Olivia. Mandie liked to bounce the word around like it was a game of catch between friends. *I love that Lenny Kravitz song. I love that new Thai place on the corner. I love that hat on you.* Olivia didn't feel love for much of anything, other than maybe her walks on the beach.

Andrew waited for her response. Olivia wanted to please him, but she just couldn't pull out the words. Fortunately, she had worked up a good froth of toothpaste in her mouth, so she said it . . . but not quite.

"I muv ew ooo," she said, lifting her eyebrows to suggest a smile.

He hugged her from behind and returned to the kitchen. She could hear him hum as he washed the dishes. Once dressed, she grabbed her bag and headed out the door, "Lock up when you're done!" she called to him, feeling a sense of relief that she was leaving. She could feel their relationship dying, not that it had ever had much life, but she didn't have the energy to end it herself.

Chapter 4

Brad's bike split the evening air, the familiar drone of his Harley growling in his ears. He picked up speed, feeling the thrill of liberation as he pushed his bike way beyond the legal limit.

The Loop was a famous stretch of back roads forty-five miles south of Saint Augustine, loved by motorcyclists for its curvy swamp-side roads and wooded trails lined with ancient oaks and palms. As Brad sped down the road, he couldn't help but feel as if he were journeying, not through the Florida backwoods, but through a dark, enchanted forest.

The sun was just setting over the salt marshes, causing the long shadows of hanging moss to look like the long fingers of hungry giants looming from above. Below, the ripples of the cool water pulsed.

Brad told everyone that he was happiest on his bike, and up until a few years ago he was. *Better than sex,* he always professed, but what he didn't say was that lately, since his almost fatal motorcycle accident seven years earlier, he felt the pleasure waning.

Less than a decade earlier, a semi-trailer had sideswiped him on Interstate 95, sending his body sliding across the asphalt, his skin peeling like a potato at seventy miles per hour. As he lay on the highway, immobilized, his mind flitting in and out of consciousness, he had stared up at the cloud-covered sky and decided his life would soon be over. He was a dead man.

But someone had seen him and called for help. The ambulance had arrived and pulled him from the highway, and somehow the doctors had put him back together. The pain of a broken hip and shattered femur had been excruciating, demanding months of intense physical therapy that felt more like medieval torture than modern medicine.

He always thought that coming back from near death would bring him a new lease on life, but instead it left him feeling dull. It was almost as if he left his life back on that highway, years ago. Even encounters with desirable girls, like Courtney, brought him little satisfaction these days. He kept searching, thinking that one of the random women found at a bar would awaken him. Fucking girls always worked briefly, but in the end he returned to emptiness.

Brad played with the curves in the road, swishing and swaying, trying to illicit that playful delight he had felt when he'd first gotten this new bike, but the joy never came. He turned off on US1 and headed towards the White Eagle Bar.

It was just about dark when Brad pulled into the parking lot. Sounds from the opening band came from the rundown one-story building that looked more like a two-hundred-year-old frontier outpost than a bar. Brad backed his bike into a parking spot.

He stepped into the bar. The smell of booze and dark leather filled the space. Although he never saw himself as a follower, he fit right in with his leather vest, boots, and his skull-adorned doo rag—almost a uniform in places like this.

It was early and the crowd was subdued. While scouting out for his friends, an unfamiliar man approached him with a drunken grin on his face.

"Hey, Brad-man! How's it going?"

"Not bad," Brad said, furrowing his brow with his lack of recognition.

"I'm Rob!" the thirty-something man said, gesturing to himself. It still didn't ring a bell.

Rob lifted his shirt to reveal a chest-sized skull tattoo adorned with hibiscus flowers. Brad recognized the ink instantly.

"Yeah! It looks good," Brad said. He mused at the fact that he recognized his ink more than he did his customers.

From the back of the bar, Brad saw a familiar woman, white hair piled on her head, a River Grill tank top on, waving her arms wildly at Brad. Dog was beside her, carrying a whiskey and a beer in each hand. Brad excused himself from Rob and headed over to his friends.

"Hey, buddy!" Dog said, giving his pal a strong hug and a pat on the back.

Suze, Dog's counterpart, his second wife, hugged him and gave him a kiss on the cheek.

"You're looking trim and healthy," Suze said, patting Brad's belly.

Dog chuckled, "Not bad for an old man, eh?"

Brad had just had his fifty-first birthday. He was twelve years younger than Dog and Suze and took pride in the fact that beer drinking didn't go to his gut.

"You been here long?" he asked, speaking over the music.

"We've been here three whiskeys long," Suze said, holding up a shot glass in a mock toast and downing it.

Dog's wife was a big drinker. Dog liked to keep up with her, but he'd been warned by his doctor to stay off the sauce. Of course, that didn't stop him. Dog's interpretation of the doctor's request was to stick to beer instead of hard liquor, but he rarely followed his own rule as well.

"Let's get you a beer, boy!" Dog yelled over the band. He turned to a bartender with globe-size breasts and said, "A Budweiser for my friend here!" The girl looked Brad's way and she gave him a wink. Brad smiled back.

Dog noticed and started laughing. He stepped close to Brad and spoke in his ear.

"You do realize she's, like, Courtney's age?"

Brad had a flash to the night before, as he pounded his best friend's granddaughter in the tattoo chair. Brad knew he could never tell Dog about Courtney. If he did, it would kill him. In fact, on Courtney's first day of work Dog had pulled Brad aside and sternly said, "Don't do her."

Courtney was his only granddaughter and, regardless of how she conducted herself in the shop, she was still his innocent little flower.

Brad joked about the big-breasted girl. "This girl is what? Twenty-one, twenty-two?" Brad said. "I've done younger. Fair game in my book."

Dog laughed and ran his fingers through his beard. "No, you're wrong. I'm thinking that one is just two weeks shy of jail bait." He turned to the girl. "How old are you, honey?" he asked.

"I turned eighteen last month." She smiled.

The men laughed and toasted their drinks. The band started a cover of a Led Zeppelin tune and Suze perked up.

"They're playing my song!" she said, grabbing Dog's hand.

"Hold on, babe. Hold on," Dog said, tossing down a shot of Jack before he followed his wife to the dance floor. As the two stepped and twisted, Suze gestured to Brad to join them, but he just shook his head with a smile. There was no way in hell they would get him out there. She brushed him off and started twisting her hips to the tune.

Brad tapped his foot and watched his friends, married twenty-five years, move away in a tipsy dance of seduction. As he watched, he felt something that he couldn't quite place. It wasn't exactly longing or even jealousy, just an empty space within him. He didn't know what it was, nor did he want to. He grabbed another beer.

As he paid for his drink, a bleached-blond woman tapped him on the shoulder. Her hair was big, reminiscent of the way his ex used to wear hers in the Eighties. Her eyeliner was laid on so thick she had almost a panda-like quality to her, but this wasn't enough to distract him from the tight skirt that clung to her hips.

"I like the tat," she said over the music. She was pointing to the one on his forearm. Her black top was cropped just above her mid-section revealing just the right amount of skin to make any healthy man want to see more.

"Thanks," he said.

"Does it mean anything?" she asked, touching his skin.

"It's a phoenix. It's sort of my thing." He took a swig of his drink.

"There's got to be a story, right?"

"Yeah." Brad looked into her eyes, holding the gaze long enough to make her glance away. It was a trick he'd used so often it had become more sport than an act of seduction.

He continued, "I had a motorcycle accident and spent nine months in rehab. After that I was drawn to the story of the phoenix."

He gestured to Dog who was doing some strange grooving motion with his hips. "If it wasn't for my buddy, Dog, over there pushing my ass out of bed every day, I probably wouldn't be walking. The phoenix is sort of a reminder of where I've come. I even named my tattoo shop the Phoenix." That part just about always piqued their interest.

"Oh yeah? In Saint Augustine?" She asked, very interested now. "My sister got the one on her ankle done there. That's your shop?" This time she looked back at him and held his gaze.

"Yep. You want a drink?" he asked.

"Yeah, sure. Bud Lite."

Brad ordered a beer and brought it back to the girl. "I'm Brad, by the way," he said.

"Catalina," she said, holding her long painted nails forward to shake his hand.

"Hey, it's really loud in here. Wanna step outside?" he said over the music.

"Sure!"

His moratorium on women would have to wait. Catalina would be an easy lay.

He lead her past a gang of scraggly, grey-haired men wearing jackets adorned with Knights of the Inferno patches and took her to the back lot behind the bar.

In the open field sat several unused outdoor bars and an abandoned stage, used only for big bike events. Catalina wobbled in her heals, giggling in a drunken stupor as he helped her up onto the stage.

There was no question in either of their minds where this was going. Within moments, his hands were on her breasts, her skirt pushed up, and he was mounting her with force.

When Brad finished, he rolled off. He didn't speak, just stared at the little pin pricks of light that made it through the darkness of the night sky.

Catalina turned to him and affectionately played with his ear. "How was it for you?" she asked in a sloppy bedroom voice.

There was a silent pause as Brad's eye followed a shooting star.

"Fine," he said.

Catalina, dissatisfied with his response, pulled her purse over her shoulder, and stood. Just before she climbed off the stage she paused, looking towards the front of the bar.

"What's going on there?" she asked.

Brad looked behind him and noticed red and blue strobing lights illuminating the parking lot. A crowd of people were watching an ambulance.

His phone vibrated three times in his pocket and he reached for it.

There were three messages, all of them from Suze.

"Something is wrong with Dog."

"Where are you?"

"We're headed to Flagler Hospital."

Brad brought himself to standing too quickly and steadied himself on a rail. Catalina looked at him, confused.

"You okay?" she asked.

He didn't answer. He just buttoned his jeans and jumped off the stage.

As he rushed to the parking lot, it felt like his boots were weighed down with lead. He was trapped within his own panic. By the time he reached the lot, all he could do was watch helplessly as the ambulance drove away.

Chapter 5

The girl with pink cotton-candy hair shifted her lithe body on the stage, jutting her fringe covered breasts forward. She cocked her head back, exposing her long neck, and froze, grinning to a point in the back of the art studio.

Olivia took another sip of her cranberry vodka and looked over to Mandie's sketch pad. A clear likeness of the girl on stage was emerging. Olivia looked to her own picture, which by comparison was lumpy and asymmetrical—an unintentional Picasso.

Coming here was Mandie's idea. These things usually were. But as awkward as the idea of a burlesque-themed life drawing class at Flagler College felt to Olivia, she was willing to try it. With a few mixed drinks in her, she might even have some fun.

Dr. Sketchy's Anti-Art School was a craze started in New York and spread to venues all over the country. Men and women, cutting-edge artists, and art enthusiasts arrived to liquor up and share their fondness for sexual fantasies blended with their love of the creative process.

When the first modeling session was complete, another woman, this time wearing the scant suggestion of a Bo Peep costume, came on stage, dragging with her a man dressed as a sheep. The woman positioned herself on a tall swing hanging from the ceiling and the sheep climbed himself on top of her, grinning at the audience as he straddled her, proud of the prize lady he was mounting. The audience of artists and curious onlookers cheered as the two began swinging across the stage.

"So you think Andrew would dress in a sheep costume for you?" Mandie asked as she made a fresh line on a new piece of paper.

"Noo . . ." Olivia said, then she paused. "Actually, I don't know. But do you really think *I'd* be into that?"

"I don't know. What are you into? You never talk about it," Mandie said as she drew a swooping arch for Bo Peep's bonnet.

"I dunno. Is it possible to not be into anything?" She paused. "I know you think it's not going good between Andrew and me, but it's fine. There's no need to complicate it with sheep costumes," Olivia said with a smirk.

"But *is* your relationship fine?" Mandie asked, looking at her friend who had barely marked her paper.

Olivia sighed.

"Come on Livia, tap into that inner you. Let it all out," Mandie said.

"Well, yeah. I guess sometimes I'm just not feeling it," she confessed as she looked around at the other artists to see if anyone was listening. They were all distracted by the fairytale antics on stage.

"You want the honest truth, Mand? I'm just not *excited*. Don't get me wrong, he's a great guy, right?"

"Yes, Andrew is very nice," Mandie said.

"But I'm feeling like a dead fish. I have no interest in sex."

Bo Peep and her sheep repositioned themselves. The pantalooned girl gave the sheep a whap on his butt with her cane.

Mandie and Olivia returned to their conversation.

"What about toys?" Mandie asked. Her eyes lit up as she spoke." Oh! I just got the most amazing dildo! Tank and I call him Silicon Steve. It's got like…"

"Yeah, okay." Olivia interrupted. "I don't need to learn about sex toys. I tried the one you recommended . . . you know . . . the *vibrator*," Olivia said, muttering the word like it was profanity.

"That one you picked up at Melissa's Intimates? That's kid's stuff. You need power tools, sista! We need to do a trip to Nuts and Bolts."

"Mandie, I don't think it's the lack of fist-size dildos in my life that's the problem. I suspect there's something fundamentally wrong with me. I mean, you know, I've never been super thrilled about *it*."

"You're blocked! You're scared. You're afraid of letting go." She paused and gave her friend a sympathetic look. "Maybe you're with the wrong guy."

Olivia bit her lip.

Mandie continued, "I mean, you know as well as I do that you're all gridlocked in there. You've got to face the fact that Andrew has never *moved* you. He's never helped unblock you."

Olivia began intensely erasing a pencil line as the crowd rose to excitement when a man sporting a puffy goatee and wearing lederhosen and fishnets jumped on stage and began pretending to mount the sheep-boy from behind. The group cheered him on as Bo Peep appeared to be figuring out a way to join in.

Mandie, now distracted by the on-stage theatrics, returned to her sketch pad.

The obscene actions on stage and the noise from the jeering crowd made Olivia feel queasy. She took a long sip of her drink.

Olivia had put eight months into Andrew and had told herself for quite some time that he was the one. She resisted the burgeoning tears.

Olivia looked at the clock on the back wall. Eight thirty. She was supposed to meet Andrew in fifteen minutes at A1A Ale Works down the street. She placed her eraser and charcoal into a case and snapped it shut, then flipped her oversized sketch book closed and tucked it under her arm.

"Where are you going? There's three more models," Mandie said.

"I'm supposed to meet Andrew," Olivia said as Harry Potter in a black leather gag came on stage, his white ass poking out from behind his cape. "I promised him we'd do drinks tonight."

"What are you going to tell him?" Mandie asked.

"What do you mean?" Olivia looked at her blankly.

"I mean, are you going to break up with him?"

"No . . . I mean, I can't. Not now."

"Okay . . . when you're ready."

Olivia felt the tears budding in her eyes again.

"Oh, hon," Mandie said in a sympathetic tone. "I'm sorry."

"I know things with Andrew aren't so good," Olivia said. "But I really wanted this one to work."

"Olivia, hon, you're at a crossroads. You can take one path and keep doing what you've always done . . . you're safe but not happy; or, you can take the other route, which is an absolute mystery. I mean, this path is dark. You have no idea what's in store, good or bad. All you know is that if you take it, you'll find change—big change."

Olivia watched her friend—the same incompetent one who came to work stoned and neglected to pay the bills, yet in that moment she was a beautiful, pin-curled goddess.

"You'll make the right choice, I know," Mandie said.

Olivia wiped her eyes and smiled.

"Go see your man, then go home, make some tea, put your feet up, and I'll see you in the morning."

In order to get to the restaurant from Flagler College, Olivia had to walk east towards the Matanzas River through the Plaza de la Constitución, the nation's oldest park. For hundreds of years, the spot functioned as a meeting place, a bustling center in the ancient city. At night the tall oaks with their ancient Southern charm hung overhead, the sagging mosses like a canopy custom built to shelter drunken college students and homeless men who sought comfort below.

As Olivia walked through the park's center, she noticed a young woman walking towards her at a rapid pace. Preoccupied, the girl veered into Olivia, bumping her shoulder as she passed. Olivia looked at her, confused. Before she could make sense of what had happened, a guy in a hoodie stepped up and grabbed Olivia by her shoulders. In a panic she tried to run.

"No. Hold still," he said as he held her there. Two other guys, one with a portable stereo, came from behind. She backed away anticipating the worst.

The girl was standing tall now, hands on her hips. She shouted loud enough to echo through the park, "One! Two! Three!"

Olivia was sure she was going to have a gun jabbed in her back, but when the man's stereo began to play Andrew's favorite—*My Everything*, by Barry White—she looked to her left and noticed another girl approaching her with a video camera.

The violins on the stereo began. A deep, mellow voice filled the space below the trees. The guys began shaking their hips in a mock disco style when twenty more people came from all sides of the park, some dressed as bums, others as tourists and college students, spinning and pirouetting like a Broadway musical come alive.

Then, from the depths of the group a familiar face emerged. He wasn't wearing his regular bow tie, but instead wore his favorite plaid shirt, his hair spiked up into a faux- hawk as if he was going for a night on the town.

Andrew looked at Olivia, his hands shaking, perspiration on his brow. He gave her a loving smile and suddenly his scrawny body appeared to bellow out the dark, sweet tones of a large black man.

In you I've found so many things
A love so new, only you could bring . . .

He lip synced, gesturing towards her with sweeping motions as the crowd behind him flashed their hands, dancing to the rhythm with theatrical grins across their faces.

Can't you see it's you? You make me feel this way
You're like a first morning dew on a brand new day

Then, as the violins faded into the back ground, Andrew, out of breath, lowered down to one knee. Olivia's heart sank.

"Olivia, when I'm with you I feel whole. You're my security blanket on a stormy night, my comfort in an otherwise blustery day. I want to hold on to you, Olivia, keep you by my side, have you 'til death do us part."

There were a few hoots from the group.

A guy dressed as an old man, who Olivia now recognized as Dave, one of Andrew's colleagues at the college, stood up from a bench and handed Andrew a small felt-covered box. Andrew opened it and held it towards her.

Though the park was dim, she could make out a small diamond on an antique band.

With a waver in his voice he asked, "Olivia Parker, will you marry me?"

Olivia sensed in her periphery a video camera focused tight on her face and suddenly didn't feel so well. Her stomach rolled and it seemed as if hundreds of stars were surrounding her vision. She was about to faint.

"I've got to sit down," she said, faltering to the bench. Feeling the weight of the curious eyes on her, Olivia took slow, deep breaths, wishing her exhalations could push away the moment.

She turned to Andrew, whose anxious petting of her left arm was doing nothing to calm her. His eyes were focused on her face, hope emanating from his pores.

She looked at him with teary eyes. "Andrew, I just can't do this," she said. "I can't keep faking this. I . . . I . . . don't love you." And, as she said this, she could feel the crowd pull back.

Andrew looked at her, confused.

Olivia continued, "Why would you put me in front of all these people and video cameras? This is awful. Really, really awful."

She stood up. The crowd divided in silence, creating a path for Olivia. Her feelings were messy, chaotic, crippling. Not knowing what else to do she started to run, her flip flops acting as a metronome to her desolate tune.

Olivia had no plan. Home was just around the corner, but she needed to be outside, where the calming night air could soothe her.

In the distance, through her watery vision, she saw the Bridge of Lions, a drawbridge across the Matanzas River that led travelers out of the old city on a pathway to the ocean. Unlike the solidity of the old city, beach life was impermanent, constantly upturned by the tides. In the ocean, fresh starts happened with each moment. Olivia felt its pull.

Guarding the bridge's entrance stood two marble lions, fifteen feet tall on pedestals of stone. Though she saw them every day on her walk to work, today, in her raw state, Olivia found their silence comforting. She crossed the empty street and approached one lion on the south side of the street. Guided by its stoic power, she moved towards it, reaching up and rubbing her hand against its stone paw.

As she looked upward, captivated by its smooth, twisting mane, a large osprey, feathered in grey and white, circled overhead. Cupping its wings, the creature descended, perching itself on the head of the other beast.

The bird gave Olivia a sideways glance, let out a series of high-pitched cries, and then flew off. Olivia's eyes remained on the lion across the street until she noticed nestled at the foot of the lion was a small wooden box.

Feeling drawn to this out-of-place object, she stepped into the street, completely unaware of the approaching motorcycle that shot over the bridge.

Chapter 6

By the time Brad noticed the woman crossing the street, it was too late. All he could do was swerve his bike to avoid her. In a controlled slide, he landed fifteen feet beyond her, the bike leaning sideways as it traveled, placing pressure the whole way along his left leg. When the bike finally stopped, he heard a woman's voice.

"Oh, my God! I am so sorry. I didn't see you coming." She looked more shaken up than he felt. "Are you okay?"

"I'm fine," Brad said, killing the engine then leveraging the bike enough to pull his leg out.

He stood slowly to see a thin, mousy, brown-haired woman in a baggy t-shirt and tan shorts standing there, looking at him with concern.

"I'm so very sorry. I can't believe I didn't see you." She walked towards him.

"Oh, you're bleeding!" She gasped. "Oh, geez. I'm really, really so sorry."

He looked down to see the side of his arm dripping blood. His adrenaline was still going and he didn't even feel the sting.

"Here. Let me help you," she said, reaching into her green handbag and pulling out a handful of tissues. "Sit down," she said, ushering him to the curb below one of the lions.

"This is just awful. I can't believe this," she mumbled to herself, dabbing his wound. He winced.

"Oh, geez. I'm sorry. I'm not much of a nurse." She looked into his warm eyes. "Maybe you should do this." She handed him the tissue.

She watched closely as he dabbed at a cut on his palm, noting a collage of well-crafted tattoos, the centerpiece of his forearm being a fiery bird in oranges and reds.

"I hope you can forgive me," she said, entranced by the images on his skin. "Are you going to be okay?"

Brad laughed. "I'm okay. I've had a lot worse. Trust me." He paused and looked right at her, his blue eyes meeting her green. "I didn't even ask, are you okay?"

"It wasn't me who crashed my motorcycle. I'm fine."

She cringed as he pulled a piece of asphalt from his palm.

"This has been one big, crappy day," she said, tears forming in her eyes.

"Yeah, no shit," Brad said, standing abruptly in hopes of escaping whatever sad story the girl was about to tell.

"I need to get going. Someone's expecting me," he said, but as he stood he felt his body teeter, his orientation of up and down, right and left unclear. He dropped himself back to the curb and put his head in his hands.

"Holy crap." He breathed deep.

"You need to rest," the girl said.

She looked over at the bike lying on its side, far enough over that any incoming car wouldn't hit it.

"I hope I didn't ruin your motorcycle . . ."

"It's just scratched," he said, his head still in his hands.

"I'm so sorry," she said again.

He looked up. "You can stop saying that. I'm fine."

"Yeah?" she asked, imploring him.

"Yeah."

She looked out over the water and spoke. "This has been the worst night ever."

He laughed. "Me, too," he said. "But, you know, I like to tell myself that bad things happen for a reason. Something good always comes from it." His words were more convincing than his expression as he groaned while repositioning his banged-up leg.

She kept her eye on him. "I suppose that could be true, but right now I'm not feeling it."

"Yeah." He grinned. "Me neither."

"You know why all this happened?" she asked.

"No, why?" he gave her a curious look.

The woman rose and walked over to the stone lion that stood fifteen feet tall behind them. Brad watched in confusion as she placed her foot in a groove at the base of the statue and lifted herself up, straining to reach a brown, rectangular object resting beside its paw. She brought herself down and settled next to Brad again.

The box was roughly six inches long and made of a dark wood, its reddish-brown stain almost completely worn away. Metal reinforcing tabs, each embossed with a small flower, were tacked into each corner. She rotated the box in her hand, appreciatively gazing at the vine-like pattern adorning the edges. Along one side, etched in intricate lettering, were the words: *non plus chaos*.

"That was just sitting there under the statue?" Brad asked.

"Yeah. That's why I was crossing the street," she said, still turning the box in her hands.

"What do the words mean?"

"Chaos… something. I don't know. I never studied Latin," she said as she slowly traced the words with her index finger.

"Here." She handed the box to him.

"What do you want me to do with it?" he asked, refusing to take it.

"Open it." She pushed it forward again. "I want to know what's in it."

"Then you should do it."

"No, I insist." She gave him a little smile and pushed it towards him again.

"All right, but if there's treasure inside, it's yours. Finders keepers."

"No way. I got you and your bike all beat up."

"How about this? Whatever is in there, we split it?"

"Deal."

He shook it a couple of times, then unhinged the clasp, but before opening it he paused and looked at the woman. She smiled at him, wide eyed, with an innocence that warmed him.

"Go on," she said, and he returned his attention to the box. He lifted the lid.

To their disappointment it was empty.

"Nothing," he frowned.

She shrugged. "Bummer."

As he re-latched the box, a low sound reverberated as if the bridge itself was calling out, deep and eerie.

"Did you hear that?" she asked.

"Yeah. Probably just an alligator in the river. They make some strange sounds during mating season."

She looked quizzically at this rough-looking man, thinking he must be some kind of fool to think an alligator would make a noise like that.

"I didn't know alligators made sounds," she said.

"They do." He handed her the box. "Here. It's yours now. Maybe one of the museums in town can explain it. I dunno. Either way, it looks like a good mystery for you, Nancy Drew."

The echoing sound returned and the blood left her face.

"Relax," Brad said. "He's probably out there horny as hell, looking for some hot alligator chick. He's got no interest in you." He eyed her. "I mean no offense . . ." He sized her up. "You've got, what? Sort of a *Gilligan's Island* Marianne thing going." He grinned. "Yeah, an alligator isn't going to go for you."

He rose slowly and walked with a stiff limp to his bike. He grunted as he lifted the eigft-hundred-fifty-pound Harley, raised his leg over the seat, and sat down. She watched him from the curb as he turned the ignition and revved the engine.

"See. Still works," he said.

She observed him, a hint of sadness in her eyes.

"Well, it's been . . . nice, but I really need to get going."

She held her unhappy gaze.

"My friend is in the hospital." Brad paused. "I need to say 'Hi.' "

"Okay," she said softly.

She glanced back to the plaza as if unsure of what she was going to do with herself, not just that in the moment, but for the rest of her life. A look of desperation manifested itself in her tired eyes.

"Hey, you okay?" he asked over the growl of his Harley.

"Yes. Fine. Thanks," she said, despondent.

"Okay . . ." he said. But, just as he shifted into gear he called to her.

"Maybe I'll see you around."

"Yeah. Maybe," she said, and she watched him speed off down the street.

Chapter 7

Olivia watched the man ride past the plaza. As he reached the midway point of the park she noticed a grey, smoky silhouette that seemed to be trailing behind him. She watched, perplexed, as this shadow-like form followed him, vague and undefined like an uncertain fog.

The sound of the man's motorcycle faded into a dull drone as the man and the strange shadow retreated into the darkness.

Olivia lifted the box and rotated it in her hands, noting its refined, delicate craftsmanship and wondering how something so beautiful could just be left there. She opened it again and rubbed her finger along the red velvet lining.

The sound from the water returned. This time it was less like an animal and more like a human in the midst of a fit of laughter. This was no alligator.

Olivia turned to the river, hoping to find the source, when she had the sense that someone—or something—was with her. A smoky shadow, just like the one she had seen following the man, was now hovering beside her.

The laughter returned, and she felt her body stir as if her insides were awakening. As the sound continued, it seemed that the noise itself was loosening the tension within her chest. The muscles around her spine, normally tense, relaxed and she found herself lightening, becoming buoyant and airy. The weight of her troubled evening seemed to float away, leaving her potent and powerful.

Without thought, she placed the box in her bag and headed back through the plaza towards home. Her mind no longer dwelled on her failed romance, the strange shadow, or the accident she had caused; it was now directed to the simple beauty of Saint Augustine at night. She marveled at a vine draped along an ancient stone wall, the tickle of a breeze against her downy arms.

She climbed the stairs to her apartment and became intensely aware of the funny squeaking sound her wooden stairs made as she stepped on them. Pausing for a moment, she rocked back and forth on the foot boards, letting the *eek, eek, eek* squawk in a playful rhythm.

Inside her apartment, everything seemed to have a magical sheen as if pixies had decorated it with fairy dust. In her strange stupor, she dropped her bag on the couch and wandered to the bathroom where she found her tired but smiling reflection in the mirror.

Behind her, she noticed the shadow. It had followed her and was now watching her, its face an abyss of darkness. Though she knew she should have been terrified, she wasn't.

"Are you doing this?" she asked.

The creature laughed.

Unconcerned, she got herself ready for bed and climbed under the covers and drifted off, sleeping better than she had in years.

Chapter 8

Brad found Courtney sitting in the hospital waiting room and staring blankly at a TV screen. Her nails were chewed to the quick. When she saw Brad, she stood up and wrapped her arms around him.

"I'm so glad you're here!" she said.

"What happened?" he asked

"Gramps had a *minor cardinal infraction*. That's what the doctor said, anyway."

"Myocardial infarction," he corrected her. He knew the term well from when his own grandpa had had one many years ago. But *his* had killed him.

"He just had surgery," Courtney said. "He's in recovery, right now. Suze said she tried to get a hold of you, but you didn't answer."

"Where is she?"

"She's grabbing a coffee at the cafeteria. She'll be back soon," Courtney said, and then, noticing the scrape on his face, she reached to touch it.

"What happened to you?"

He pulled back.

"I'm fine, just had a little accident."

"Did you get into a fight?" she asked, concerned.

Brad shook his head. He hadn't been in a fight since he was twelve.

"No. I had a spill on my bike, but I'm fine."

"You don't look fine…" Courtney said.

"I am," Brad answered.

Courtney, ignoring Brad's obvious need for space, brought herself towards him and laid her head on his shoulder.

"Is he going to die?"

Brad consoled her with a hasty pat, his body rigid and stiff.

"Dog? You kidding? Nothing can take that man down."

His words did no good. She sobbed loudly until her tears soaked the shoulder of his t-shirt.

He pulled away and adjusted his shirt so that the snot didn't sit quite so heavy on his arm and turned back to the TV, as if the activity on that particular episode of *Jeopardy* was more important than the situation at hand.

Alex Trebek spoke through the tinny TV speakers: "The first human woman in Greek mythology to be created by the gods."

"Who is Pandora?" Brad said in unison with the male contestant on the show.

Courtney gave him a confused look.

He ignored her and kept watching the screen until from somewhere behind him he heard a low growl. It was similar to the growl at the bridge, but this seemed to be more drawn out—a low rumble, articulated by slow huffs, almost like demonic laughter.

"Did you hear that?" he asked.

"Hear what?" she asked.

"That laughing . . . like a man." He glanced around the room. "Where is it coming from?"

He looked around the lobby, paranoia seething.

Go away! he thought to himself, his heart picking up speed. The laughter continued with a roar. Whatever this was, it wasn't just a disembodied sound, but something dark and hungry mocking his weakness.

"Brad?" Courtney looked at him. "You okay?" She delicately touched his hand.

Brad recoiled.

"Don't touch me!"

"Dude, you're in bad shape," Courtney said, puzzled by his sudden lack of composure.

"I'm . . . fine, " he stammered, his eyes shifting back to the TV as if he could just wish the dark laughter away, but the sound continued. Crazed, he looked around the waiting area. Then, stunned, he spotted it, hovering behind his shoulder, a shadowy body shifting and flowing within itself like a living vapor, sentient and wise.

"I need to go, Courtney. Tell Dog I'll be back, okay?"

"Brad, what's going on with you?" Courtney asked, giving him a concerned look, but before he even heard her, he was out the door and on his bike.

Chapter 9

Thursday morning, Olivia's energy was bright and wild. She was itching for stimulation, wanting to savor every little detail of life.

Thinking she might stop by a local museum and do some research on the box, she double checked to make sure it was still in her bag.

Olivia left the house and headed down Aviles Street towards the plaza on the same route she followed every morning, but today things were different. The world felt softer and friendlier than it had before. The streets were alive in vibrant, living colors. She felt as if she were bathing in the sounds of singing birds, the town's living energy permeating her skin.

She walked down the cobblestone road, stopping at a store window, captivated by rows and rows of confections: fudges, cherry cordials, caramels, pecan clusters. As she gazed at the glass, she noticed her own reflection overlaying the chocolate delights.

This was not the Olivia she knew. She appeared so light and airy that she could take off and fly within the clouds. There was no conflict, no constant worries in her mind. Just joy.

When she arrived at Eat it Too, she put on her apron and began the morning routine: measuring oil, buttermilk, and sugar into each of the industrial-sized mixers and letting them run.

She went to the shop's old answering machine, which was coated in a fine dusting of flour, and pressed play. It was Mandie.

"Hey girl, Pogo's got the runs. I have to take him to the vet. I'll be about an hour late today."

On most days, Mandie's lame alibi would have irritated Olivia to no end, but today she found herself amused with her friend's ridiculous excuses.

Olivia walked over to Mandie's iPod and started the music. Mic Jagger, with his wild, slurred speech, shouted:

Pleased to meet you.
Hope you guess my name.

And though The Stones had never been Olivia's preference, somehow the rhythm struck her this morning. She sifted the flour into the mixer, shaking her hips to the rhythm of the drums.

As the mixture formed, she devilishly dipped two fingers into the batter and licked them clean, letting the sweet batter slide down her throat with mischievous pleasure.

How odd, she thought, that she had worked in this bakery for so long and had never even stolen a little lick for fear of added calories. She shrugged, took another taste, and then headed to the front to sweep.

Ten o'clock came. The cupcakes were cooled and frosted, but Mandie was nowhere in sight.

Olivia flipped the front sign to "Open" and propped the front door wide, welcoming the tourists who would soon be streaming down Saint George Street, following the scent of the town's only collection of macabre baked goods.

She put on a clean apron and placed the Quoth the Raven cupcakes gently into the large glass case. The smell of peanut butter drifted her way and, like a werewolf at the full moon, she felt herself weaken. She quickly shut the case and stepped away. She may have had some sort of odd awakening overnight, but Olivia still knew that those cupcakes were easily four hundred calories each—one quarter of the calories she allotted herself each day.

As she distracted herself with menial cleaning jobs, Olivia heard the grinding roll of a skateboard approaching. She looked outside to see a guy, maybe ten years younger than herself, stop across the street. The shadow's laughter began again.

Olivia's eyes were drawn to this man, a specimen from a different world. His t-shirt was off, tucked in at his waistline, his bare chest exposed, his scraggly hair hanging in his eyes. Nothing about this vagrant surfer kid should have been sexually appealing, yet she kept watching him, taking in his every detail; the smoothness of his skin, his tousled, sun-bleached hair, his cool, uncaring posture.

He removed his backpack and sat down on a bench so nonchalant, so carefree and comfortable that it stirred something peculiar in Olivia. She wanted *that*. Not just the guy, but the freedom he possessed.

Not quite in control of herself she reached into the bakery case and placed a red velvet Bleeding Heart cupcake onto a plate and then stepped onto the narrow street. The laughter began again, echoing off of the city's ancient brick buildings.

She spotted the shadow now standing in the midst of the morning crowd. People were completely oblivious to it, several of them walking right through it, unaware of its smoky presence. The movements of the crowd didn't even stir the beast. It was focused on Olivia, and Olivia alone.

It laughed again, and Olivia felt herself soften once more.

Detached from her actions, she spoke: "Hi there. I saw you here and I was wondering…"

She brought the plate forward.

"Do you like cupcakes?" she asked with a wide smile.

"Yeah. You just giving them away?"

"Sure. You look like the kind of guy who appreciates a little sweetness in the morning," she said with an unfamiliar coyness.

He looked at her with his dark brown eyes and smiled.

"Thanks." He took the cupcake from the plate, peeled back the paper, and brought it to his mouth. His lips, still curved in a smile, folded around the cake. She watched him with a surprising amount of pleasure, focused on a silver lip ring that arched like a crescent moon around his bottom lip. She had the odd desire to wrap her tongue around it.

"Oh you've got a little on your lip," she said as she leaned over and wiped the frosting from the corner of his mouth.

He stepped back in surprise, but kept on smiling.

"I'm Jesse." He pulled a few stray hairs from his face and continued to look at her.

"I'm...."

Olivia paused, unable to recall her own name. She blinked at him several times, and then turned quickly into the store, closing the door behind her.

What the hell did I just do there? she thought in a panic. She stepped into the privacy of the back kitchen and settled herself in a big desk chair.

"Deep breaths. Deep breaths," she told herself, trying to regain control of her heated body.

Then, as her heart returned to an even pace, she watched the shadow slip through the wall into the room. It glanced at her then settled itself in the middle of the space, grey smoky wisps hanging at its side like forgotten limbs.

The shadow stared her down with its empty blackness and Olivia returned the gaze, wondering how something so foreign could also feel so familiar. It felt as if this thing, for better or worse, had always been part of her.

Without warning, the shadow drifted back through the wall, leaving Olivia alone once again. She rose slowly, moving to the counter where rows of cupcakes cooled. Without thought, without ritual, without calculation, she bit in and savored the deep chocolate delight.

At eight in the evening, Olivia flipped the sign to "Closed," grabbed her purse, and headed out the front door. She started walking towards home but stopped when she heard the sounds of a band playing down the street.

Olivia lived in a town where live musical performances were a daily occurrence, but she hadn't seen a live concert in years. Andrew had always said the loud music bothered his ears and she never refuted him because she, too, preferred the quiet comforts of home.

But, now, the rapid cadence of the bass drum snaked its way down the street, calling to her in a jungle-like rhythm that matched the pulse of her heart. Though tired from a full day of work, she turned towards the music.

Olivia followed the noise, turning left onto Hypolita Street and down to the end where Scarlett O'Hara's, one of the city's most famous restaurants, stood. The ramshackle salt-box house, typical of the area, had been expanded many times due to the ever-increasing demand of the restaurant's customers. Though well kept on the inside, its unpainted slat-board exterior gave it the feel of a home set on a Florida swamp.

The restaurant's large porches seemed as if they were about to collapse with the weight of happy revelers. Three salty-looking men, who looked like they had been playing the Saint Augustine circuit since before the Beatles finished grade school, played a playful version of *Ring of Fire* in a back corner.

Olivia climbed the stairs of the porch and waded through the people to get into the bar. On any other day, the noise of the band and shouting patrons would have been too much for Olivia, but today the sounds invigorated her, as if the cacophony of voices gave her a greater sense of awareness.

A young male bartender spotted her and called to her over the music.

"Can I get you something?"

Olivia looked at him in a daze.

"Umm . . . I don't know." She watched a plate of French fries move past her and felt herself salivate.

"I think . . . I want food," she said, surprised by her own decision. Among Olivia's many strict rules for life, one was to never eat before bedtime.

The bartender handed her a menu and pointed to a small table in the back.

She sat herself down and opened the menu. Staying true to habit, she went straight for the salad section. A cobb salad without the meat, egg, and cheese was her standard course of action.

Olivia had been a vegetarian since she was in high school, but her body in that moment begged for something with heft: fat, salt and carbs—everything she usually chose to avoid.

She flipped open the menu and paused at the listing for a bacon double cheeseburger.

She laughed to herself. This wasn't even an option in her rigid world, yet her eyes kept returning to the words on the page: *"Our bacon double cheeseburgrer is made with a hand-pressed patty, Wisconsin cheddar, and maple smoked bacon..."*

This hunger she felt was not just rooted in her stomach but in her cells, as if her very molecular structure was in need of two all-beef patties with cheese.

A short-statured waitress with ponytails and bright red streaks in her hair approached Olivia's table.

"Hi, my name is Cheri," the waitress said in an overly polite tone. "Welcome to Scarlett O'Hara's. I'll be your waitress for tonight . . ." She stopped and shifted her weight to one hip. "Sorry, they make me say that crap. Are you waiting for someone?"

Olivia looked at the empty seat.

"No . . . no. Just me."

"A single girl, huh? Me, too. I like it better that way . . . that way, I get my pick. You know what I mean?"

Olivia nodded and gave the waitress an awkward smile. She didn't know what she meant.

"So, what can I get you?"

"I would like a bacon double cheeseburger," Olivia said.

"Right on, sister! You want fries with that?"

"Uhh . . ."

"Yes. Of course you want fries." Cheri said with a smirk, writing it down.

"All right—fries! I think I'll be wild and have a glass of wine tonight, too. Chardonnay."

"You go get 'em, tiger." Cheri smiled.

A few minutes later, the waitress returned with a burger big enough to feed Olivia for a week.

"You good?" Cheri asked.

Olivia nodded and Cheri left.

As Olivia's attention focused on the cheeseburger, she heard that same fervent laughter she had heard the day before. She looked around but saw nothing out of the ordinary and returned to her overwhelming meal.

As she scooped up the bun in her hands, Olivia's body became heated and oddly aroused. She opened her mouth wide, wrapped her lips around the burger, and bit in. The meat's juices were released as a blend of dark, smoky flavors into her mouth.

Where have you been my whole life? she thought as she looked at the burger with a coy grin.

Cheri returned to her table.

"Pretty good, huh?" she asked.

"Uh huh," Olivia smiled, taking another mammoth bite.

"Well, take your time. You can pay at the bar when you're ready."

"Thanks," Olivia said, not even taking a moment to glance away from her meal. She took another bite and proceeded to eat until she felt like her belly would burst. Normally, a full stomach produced all sorts of anxiety and guilt for Olivia, but she went home that night completely satisfied.

Chapter 10

Friday at the shop was difficult for Olivia. She was antsy and anxious. Although she typically appreciated the slow days, today she just couldn't sit still. Rather than starting the new book she had picked up at Anastasia books, she found herself pacing the distance of her little shop, checking the clock compulsively, wanting nothing more than to get out. The funny thing was that she had nowhere to be. In fact, with Andrew out of her life, she had little to no social life at all, but she was itching for something—what, exactly, she had no idea. But she knew that whatever it was, it was waiting for her.

When Mandie arrived at four to take over the evening shift, Olivia barely spoke two sentences to her.

With no agenda, Olivia wandered the streets of Saint Augustine, looking in store windows, marveling at the amount of merchandise the little town offered. Tourist "crap," as she and Mandie always called it, suddenly didn't look so bad. T-shirts with idiotic slogans made her chuckle to herself. At one point, she stopped at an outdoor stand and found herself contemplating the purchase of a five-foot-high tiki carving for her front porch. She laughed it off and kept on walking.

When she reached the Ancient City Drug Store, she headed in with plans to pick up some shampoo, but as she walked down the brightly lit aisle she paused at a row of boxes, each one showing a different woman with long, flowing hair set forward, revealing hues of reds, browns, and golds.

Olivia picked up one of the boxes of hair dye and looked closely at a woman with long blond hair that swooped over her shoulders.

"Salon Quality Hair Dye Made Easy. Permanent Hair Color."

A brief moment of pleasure ran through her body as she playfully thought about dying her own hair, but she stopped herself.

No. You are not a blond. Nor will you ever be, she thought as she returned the box to its spot on the shelf.

Brunette had always been perfectly fine with her. In fact, her mom always told her she'd make a horrible blond and Olivia agreed. Dying her hair was a ridiculous idea.

"Don't rock the boat," her mom used to say. This was an idiom that Olivia had grown to live by.

Spotting the shampoos, she stepped in their direction but stopped when she noticed a cluster of faux-hair samples hanging down in three-inch locks. Fifteen color possibilities awaiting her inspection.

Following this odd, new sense of curiosity she pulled up one labeled "B5-Light Cool Breezy Blond" and held the sample up to her face. She peeked at herself in a small mirror wedged within the shelves.

This wouldn't be so bad, she thought, and she heard that detached laughter return. She looked up and saw the shadow behind her, a swirling mass of light and dark.

Olivia felt a stirring from within, as if her veins had just been infused with fire. She spotted the corresponding box of hair dye on the shelf and picked it up. The radiant model for B5 seemed to smile at her with confidence, as if telling her telepathically that dying her hair would be the most wonderful thing Olivia could do for herself.

The shadow chuckled again, and confidence took control. She moved towards the front counter, the shadow trailing behind.

A line of customers had formed there, each holding baskets brimming with their drug store finds. Olivia, feeling the welling desire to move things along, looked around anxiously, wondering if there was some other cashier who could hasten the process, but no one else was around.

The shadow let out a deep, guttural laugh again and Olivia felt an electric joy course through her body.

"Screw it!" she said out loud as she reached into her wallet and grabbed a twenty-dollar bill. Clutching the money in her hand, she stepped to the front of the line and tossed it on the counter. The cashier looked at her, confused.

"For the dye," Olivia said as she held up the box.

She walked the three blocks home filled with conviction, choosing not to question the strange shift. Climbing the stairs, she went straight to her bathroom.

She looked at her boring, lifeless hair in the mirror, pulled it behind her ears, then frowned.

"What the hell am I doing?" she asked out loud. Behind her in the refection, the shadow stood, its dark presence an abrupt contrast to the white tiled walls.

The shadow chuckled, and instantly Olivia felt that sense of excitement bubble in her veins again. She tore open the packaging with fervor. She pulled out two bottles and slipped on the accompanying gloves.

"I'm going off the deep end, I know," she said, looking at the apparition. "But, you know, I really don't care." She laughed. A warmth filled her belly. She had never felt so calm and simultaneously confident.

Olivia uncapped the two bottles and, like a chemist, she mixed the solution and the solvent together until the heat of the dye radiated through the bottle into her hands.

In her unfettered state, she began to slowly squeeze the contents of the bottle onto her scalp, drawing deliberate lines along the length of her head, the smell of ammonia forming a cloud around her.

When the bottles were empty, she wrapped a towel around her head and set the kitchen timer for twenty minutes. She situated herself on her living room couch with a book, trying to ignore the shadow's strange presence.

The timer's buzz broke the stark silence in her apartment.

Still sitting on the couch, she brought her finger to her scalp and pulled out a strand of hair from beneath the towel. Olivia brought the hair in front of her eyes.

In her hand was a gorgeous strand of honey-gold hair. An expression of sublime satisfaction came over her face as that heat she had felt at the bar built from within again and she knew she wasn't only dying her hair, she was performing a deviant act, an act of aggressive change. This new feeling—it was something she had always longed for, sensual power, strength as a sexual being.

In the shower, she watched as the amber streams of dye poured off her head and ran down her bare breasts in ribbons of gold. Stepping out, she dried her hair vigorously then looked into the mirror. Not only was she a blond, but she appeared brighter and more courageous, like her very aura had changed.

With a thick towel wrapped around her body, she walked to the kitchen to make herself some tea.

After putting a pot of water on the stove, she grabbed her purse and checked her phone messages. Normally, Andrew would be checking in, but there was nothing from him. There was, however, a text from Mandie, sent a few hours earlier.

"You left so quickly. How are you?"

Olivia paused to think about this question. She had refused her boyfriend's marriage proposal, had almost gotten run over by a motorcycle, and now she was having both auditory and visual hallucinations, but none of it seemed to hold any weight.

Olivia spoke out loud as she typed,

"I'm doing fabulous. Can't wait to show you the new look!"

Recalling the strangeness of the previous night, she pulled out the ancient wooden box she had found at the bridge and rotated it in her hands. She opened it and glided her fingers across the liner, a sensation with such supple softness that it could have been the interior of someone's soul. Then, carefully closing it, she placed it in the center of her table.

Standing, Olivia caught her reflection in the living room mirror and moved slowly towards it. Fascinated by her own foreign image, she stared into her eyes. And as she looked she oscillated between self-recognition and complete unfamiliarity, unsure of who exactly she was.

Without thought, she dropped the towel to the ground, leaving herself bare and exposed. Her eyes lingered on this body that she had always hated, resenting its shapeless, boy-like structure, but now she couldn't stop looking. There was something simple yet elegant about her subtle curves. A smile broadened across her face. She was no longer the meek girl resigned to ugly duckling status, but a golden, luscious being of light.

This beautiful self in front of her had always been there; the only difference was that now she could see it. She ran her fingers through her hair and let her hands wander past her breasts, glide over her belly, her hips, her thighs, and she smiled because she knew this was good.

At that moment, it occurred to Olivia that she was starving. All she had eaten that day were two cupcakes, and that was six hours earlier. She opened the refrigerator to find a half-eaten yogurt container and a Tupperware of cut green pepper slices.

The audible groan of her belly was all she needed to hear to make up her mind. She put on some clothes, grabbed her purse, and headed back to Scarlett O'Hara's.

Chapter 11

All day Friday, Brad went through the motions of his work day detached from the regular routine. His typical playful banter with the clients was replaced by silence, his focus only on the images he etched into their skin.

At eleven that night, he counted the till, while Buzz, the only other employee there that night, swept the floors.

"Is it okay if I stick around and finish that firefighter design?" Buzz asked.

Brad looked at Buzz, too tired to fully process his request.

"Okay. Fine . . . Just make sure you lock up when you're done."

Brad headed towards the large parking lot just north of the shop. Taking a short cut, he turned down Hypolita Street, passed Scarlett O'Hara's. The band that night had already packed up, but the tunes from the juke box were coming through the open windows, playing a song by one of his favorite bands, Black Rebel Motorcycle Club.

I'm gonna' fade your soul
I'm gonna' bleed your mind
Until you're mine
Until you're mine
Until you're mine

The heavy bass guitar and cool vocals soothed his insides.

One drink, he told himself as he stepped into the bar.

The dark oak-covered bar was filled with patrons, some at tables eating greasy bar food, others at the bar having leisurely conversations.

"Well, hi there, stranger!" said the recognizable face pulling a beer.

"Hey, Cheri. How goes it?" Brad asked.

"Just peachy, now that you're here." She gave him the same seductive glance she gave all the regulars. "What can I do ya for?"

"Yuengling," Brad said. He rested his elbow on the bar and ran his hand through his hair several times, leaving his hair twisted and wild.

Cheri slid the bottle towards him.

"So . . . how's life at the old Phoenix?"

"Well, let's see. My newest employee is a dumb ass, and I spent the whole fucking day tattooing tribal crap."

"What's wrong with tribal?" Cheri said, and she pulled one of her Doc Marten-clad feet up on the bar. A few of the other male patrons gave her a curious eye.

On her leg was a black dagger-like network of angles and curves wrapped around her calf.

Brad smiled.

"That one's not so bad, actually. But, lately, every guy and his uncle comes in my shop with some Maori/Celtic crap, thinking they're the first man on earth to put a black dragon on their shoulder blade."

Cheri put her leg down.

"Bad mood today, Brad? You're not your normal old chipper self."

He looked at her and gave her a small smile. "I'm normally 'chipper'?"

She smirked and brought him a fresh beer.

The cool alcohol spread through his insides as he drank, dulling the stress from the past few days.

"So, you have plans later tonight?" Cheri asked. "I wouldn't mind coming over to see Ghost again. He's an awesome pooch." She winked.

"That could work." Brad smiled and took another sip. Ghost always helped him get laid.

An hour and a half and four beers later, Brad struck up a conversation with a couple on their honeymoon from Atlanta. They were staying at the bed and breakfast not far from his house.

"If you're looking for things to do, don't bother with the ghost tours—go to the jail," Brad said to them.

"But, I heard Saint Augustine was one of the country's most haunted places," said the woman.

"Listen. There's no fucking ghosts in this town, unless you count the one that's been following me . . . but that's a whole other story." He laughed nervously. "Now, the Old Jail. It's great . . . they give tours of that place. In fact," Brad said. "They've got this God damned cage; freaky shit, man. You know the term 'jail bird' came from the fact they'd hang guys in cages from trees." He took another gulp of his beer.

Brad's tendency to prattle on with random history facts seemed to intensify after a few beers. The couple, who had probably never met a genuine biker before, appeared amused by his drunken lecture.

Brad kept rambling. "And those cells, I mean, man, they weren't any bigger than that bathroom over there."

He gestured with a lazy hand to the back side of the bar, and then paused when he spotted a familiar-looking girl in her late twenties sitting in a booth.

"I swear I met that chick the other night. I almost ran her over . . . but I thought her hair was brown . . ."

The couple gave Brad polite smiles and finished their glasses of wine.

Ignoring his new companions, Brad stood up and walked toward the girl but paused when he noticed someone with her—or at least that's what he thought he saw. It appeared to be a tall man, but when he got closer Brad realized he had no features. Regretting his last bottle of beer, he blinked, hoping to clear the illusion, but it remained.

Panic set in when he realized that this was the shadow he had seen at the hospital. He was sure of it, and now it sat with that woman as if it were on a dinner date with her. The creature noticed Brad looking its way, rose, and headed towards him.

Brad backed up towards the door.

"You headed home?" Cheri asked, catching him by the arm.

"Uh . . . yeah," he said.

"So . . ." Cheri said and she took his hand to keep him from slipping out. "I'll be here until one. You cool with me coming by?"

Brad looked at Cheri, then to the shadow. All he could think about was getting out that door.

"I'll have to take a rain check . . ." he said, stumbling over his own feet as he headed onto the street.

Chapter 12

Olivia entered her apartment still giddy from the two glasses of wine she had had at Scarlett O'Hara's, her belly full from her second night of greasy bar food. The shadow had been with her the whole time at the bar, but she didn't mind its presence. In fact, it seemed that when the shadow was around, the sense of anxiety that seemed to always hover over her was gone. It was like she had taken a few of Mandie's Valium, and was now reaping the benefits.

In the apartment, Olivia placed her phone in the speaker dock in the living room to give it a charge. Her radio app popped up, and a Led Zeppelin song titled *Kashmir* began spontaneously, bringing a slow, seductive pulse in the room.

The lyrics began:

Oh let the sun beat down upon my face...

It felt to Olivia as if the sun had emerged within her living room, warming her skin as silver snakes appeared to dance down the walls, leaving a trail of brightness in their wake.

Outside her window, two stories down, an older gentleman walking his dog in the late of the night paused to watch her. The thought crossed her mind that she should close the drapes, but instead she began to dance, slowly slipping off her clothes. The music continued:

I am a traveler of both time and space, to be where I have been

She closed her eyes and let the heavy guitar work pull her in, her body slowly moving with the exotic call of the violins, and she felt as if she were surrounded by the smoke and silk of a foreign land. Her body twisted to the seductive call of the violin; her heart pulsed with the short, sharp beat of the Middle Eastern drum.

My Shangri-La beneath the summer moon, I will return again...

As Olivia danced, she felt distant from her former self, her only awareness was of being pulled deep into the liberation of the moment. As she twisted and spun, she felt her whole body becoming a ravenous liquid, boiling with desire.

She continued dancing with serpent-like dexterity, letting the beat lead her on. As the rhythm crescendoed in a hot-tempered pulse, it felt as if her chest was opening up, allowing her soul—a blinding white light—to pour into the room.

The song ended, and she collapsed to the ground, breathing heavily. Her body melted into the floor, thoughts of what she was and would be passing by like boats in the fog, and she fell asleep, her cheek resting in the soft curls of the rug.

Olivia woke the next morning to sunlight streaming on her face. She groaned, slowly sat up, and then looked around the living room. Her body was sore, dehydrated, and spent. She inspected her left arm to find the red spaghetti pattern of the carpet indented on her skin. Lucy looked down on her from her perch atop the couch with a disdainful stare as if to say, "It's about time."

Olivia stood and walked towards the kitchen. The wooden box was still on the table where she had left it, but now it was open wide. She nervously looked around the room then closed the lid with a snap.

In her bedroom, Olivia peeked in the mirror and ran her fingers through her unfamiliar blond hair.

"What the hell have I done, Lucy?" she asked, looking down at her cat.

Lucy answered only by rubbing her jaw against Olivia's leg.

"I'm going nuts."

Olivia got in the shower. As the hot water pummeled her back, it felt as if the firm restraint of the past twenty-seven years of her life washed down the drain. Her life was shifting, slipping into chaos, whether she liked it or not.

Chapter 13

Brad wasn't hung over, but he might as well have been. He felt like crap. It was three ten in the afternoon, but he was just waking up now. Somehow, he had slept the day away. He rolled out of bed, pulled on a pair of jeans that were lying on his bedroom floor, and slipped on a t-shirt. As he reached for his vest, he paused to look at the patches stitched into the leather—a collection he had been adding to since the Eighties. Below the right shoulder was a dark blue one with the words "Carpe Diem" embroidered in white.

Dog had given Brad the patch when the Phoenix was just an idea. Money had been tight, then, and Brad wasn't sure he could make the business work, but one night while hanging out at Dog's and Suze's place for their weekly spaghetti dinner, Dog had pulled the patch from his pocket.

"I saw this over at the White Eagle last week, and it made me think of you," Dog said that night as he had patted Brad's shoulder. "If anybody can do this tattoo business, it's you."

He had handed Brad the patch and Brad's apprehension had dissolved. That next day Brad had placed a deposit on the storefront on Saint George Street. Within a year the Phoenix had become the most well known tattoo shop in the area.

Standing in his bedroom, Brad rubbed his face. What the hell was he doing? Dog was in the hospital, and all he could do was sit around and feel sorry for himself, paralyzed by some illusion he had created in his mind.

Less booze, he thought. He needed to get his shit together and go back to that hospital.

He arrived at Flagler Hospital late Saturday. People moved about the large lobby like it was an airport of perpetual layovers. In spite of this, the hospital was remarkably quiet.

As Brad approached the front desk, he noticed Suze coming down the hall balancing two cups of coffee and several muffins.

"Brad, I'm so glad you're here," she said as Brad took the coffees from her to relieve her load. Just as he did, the low, menacing laughter of the shadow returned, filling the open space, but rather than feeling dread, Brad felt a cool calmness slide over him.

Suze was not in good shape, but he couldn't see her pain. Her ordinarily fluffy hair was pulled back and matted, her eye makeup gone; a drained version of her jovial self, but to Brad in his altered state she was not only invincible to grief but beautiful as well. She was not the weather-worn, sixty-year-old biker chick with a husband on death's door, but something magnificent, a living work of art.

"Courtney is in there now . . . Dog has been asking about you," she said, an aura of light encircling her. "He's laying low, not talking much. He's not out of the woods, but he's awake."

"You know he's going to be just fine," Brad said, hugging her. "It's all good. . ."

"What have you been smoking?" she asked, punching him on the arm.

"Nothing," he said. "I just know all is well in the world."

Too tired to process her friend's trippy behavior, she let out a weak laugh.

"Come on, let's go see him."

Brad hated hospitals. In fact, on any other day just being there would shoot his blood pressure through the roof, but now everything felt different. The stark hospital had a sparkling glow, the nurse's carts, the food on the patients' trays, the machines that clicked and beeped as he walked by—all of it was laden with magic. To Brad, illness and death did not lurk within these hospital walls. It was a vibrant, enchanted palace.

They reached Dog's room to find him half awake. His skin was grey, his cheeks sallow, his eyes bloodshot, but his sad state didn't register on Brad. All he saw was warmth and goodness. His friend was a glorious survivor, one who had faced death and returned.

"Hey, buddy! You look great. How you feeling?" Brad said.

Dog groaned and gave Brad a weary smile.

"Been better, man," he answered.

Brad laughed.

"This place is nice," Brad said, looking around the stark room. His eyes landed on the EKG machine wired to his friend's heart.

"Holy crap. Do you realize this machine is drawing pictures of your heartbeats? That's incredible."

Dog looked at him and then to Suze.

"Whatchu been smokin', boy?" he asked, his voice weak.

"That's what I was wondering!" Suze said, laughing.

Courtney, who had been sitting in a bedside chair, added, "You should have seen Brad in the waiting room, yesterday," she said. "He was majorly flipping out."

Without thinking, Brad walked over to Courtney.

"You've got the most delicate fingers, Court."

She gave him a long smile then looked over at Suze, who was watching the two of them with a curious eye.

Dog, unaware of the too-familiar interaction, called to his granddaughter.

"Come on over here, girl. How's my angel?"

"Good, now that I'm with you." She gave him a hug. "I'm glad you're okay, Gramps."

"Of course I am. I ain't ready to leave this old world, yet. I've got to beat Brad at pool a few hundred more times before my time is up." He looked over to Brad, who was now rolling his hand over the bed sheets in awe of their texture.

"Do we need to get *you* a doctor?" Dog asked with a weak chuckle.

Brad blinked, bringing himself back into the conversation.

"No. I'm great. You're okay, so everything is good."

The disembodied laughter returned and suddenly Brad felt the euphoria slip from him and his body felt weak. The sterile smell of antiseptic stung his nostrils and he recoiled.

He looked at Dog in the bed, and the unsettling realization returned. Dog was not well. He was a sick, old man.

Brad felt the desire to run, not just from the room, but from the constant call of death and the chaos that was invading his mind.

As he backed towards the door, a doctor entered. The man couldn't have been more than five years older than Courtney.

"You must be the family," the doctor said, eyeing a patch on Brad's vest that said "Born Again Heathen." The doctor was one of those people Brad associated with public radio, veganism, and ridiculously small cars. He suddenly had the impulse to punch him.

"Yes, we're family," said Suze, taking Brad's arm and holding it tight in an effort to keep him under control.

"Mr. Struthers is healing nicely. Once we can get him stabilized, he'll be ready to go home."

Brad couldn't hear the doctor's words. He couldn't hear anything but the laughter of this evil being who seemed hell bent on taunting him.

"You know, I need to get to the shop," he said.

"Brad, please stay. You barely got here," Suze said, grabbing his arm.

The laughter persisted in Brad's head, and he became quite sure if he stayed he would collapse right onto the floor.

He backed towards the door and slipped out without saying goodbye.

Chapter 14

Brad rode towards the center of the city without a plan. All he knew was that he needed to keep himself distracted.

After arriving in downtown Saint Augustine, he parked his bike on the street.

Normally at this time of night there'd be at least two ghost tours going on simultaneously in front of the Huguenot Cemetery. The guides would be dressed in black Victorian costumes or pirate garb, depending on their flavor of tour, but today in front of the cemetery there was no one.

As he paused at the locked gate, Brad recalled overhearing a tour guide decorated with a sheriff badge and cowboy boots tell the story of Judge Eli Burnham, a prominent man in the community who died of yellow fever only to have his gold teeth stolen from his dead mouth in that very cemetery.

According to Sheriff Agin, the tour guide: "To this day, visitors see the toothless judge sitting in the trees, on the lookout for his stolen teeth." Brad remembered how the crowd had shuddered at the story.

Wrought iron fencing surrounded the eleven-acre cemetery that was shaded by oaks and sable palms. Light from neighboring street lights spilled into the yard, illuminating the weathered gravestones, causing the shadows to be long and foreboding.

As Brad gazed into the cemetery, a bird the size of a small eagle landed on one of the stone pillars at the edge of the yard. Brad had seen osprey, like this one, numerous times along the water but never up close, this deep into town.

The bird tore into a fresh fish, pausing once in a while to look down at Brad. The man and the bird stared at each other for an extended moment until the osprey became distracted by something in the trees. It cocked its head upward towards the same spot where Brad now heard a dark growl.

Brad's heart quickened. He knew what it was. The demon was lurking nearby. Brad tried to keep his focus on the osprey.

Unperturbed by the shadow, the bird looked back at Brad then ruffled her feathers. He watched as a white downy feather descended gracefully from her perch.

Brad felt the return of that cool, calm feeling he had experienced initially in the hospital as his focus became myopic, solely fixated on that tiny feather. He wanted it.

Still obstructed by the locked gate, Brad grabbed the wrought iron bars and shook them a few times to test the strength of the lock. When it didn't open, he put his foot on the bottom bar and pulled himself up, lifting a leg over the top and then landing in the darkness of the cemetery. Regaining his orientation, Brad felt a strange excitement as he searched the area.

In the grass amidst the weathered and worn gravestones was the delicate, downy feather. Brad picked it up, amazed at its undetectable weight, like an illusion resting in his hand. He looked back up to the osprey as if in thanks, but it was already gone.

As Brad returned to the edge of the graveyard, the laughter began again, deep and wild. Brad looked around, searching for its source. Up above, in one of the highest trees, sat the shadow, just like the one he had seen at Scarlett O'Hara's and at the hospital, looking down at him like a happy raven, amused by the power it held over Brad.

Brad felt his curiosity wane and panic set in. The gravestones around him, silver in the moonlight, were no longer inanimate objects, but beings, each hungry for his life.

Like a terrified child, in a blur of thought Brad scaled the fence and landed back into the safety of the well-lit street. He started towards Saint George at a brisk pace, getting himself as far away as possible from that terrible place.

The only thought on his mind being, *I need a drink.*

Chapter 15

Sunday morning at Eat it Too, Olivia stared at the antique clock that hung on the bakery wall. The old Olivia loved time. Seconds, minutes, hours. She loved the sound of the ticking of a clock dividing her day into perfect fractions. In a world that was unpredictable, time was refined and constant. But now, for some reason, time held little importance. Minutes had no meaning; it was all just moment to moment.

Mandie arrived even later than usual, but Olivia didn't care.

"Hey, sugar," Mandie called to her friend as the small bell above the door jingled.

She looked at Olivia and gasped, "What is this? What did you do?"

Olivia smiled.

"You little minx!" Mandie exclaimed. "Oh, my God. Blond?" Mandie ran up to Olivia and spun her around.

"Olivia Parker, what has gotten into you?" she smiled.

"Honestly, Mandie, I don't know. It just felt right. You like it?"

"Oh, totally. Girl, you are rockin'. I can't believe you," Mandie laughed.

Mandie slipped on one of the French maid aprons then headed to the backroom.

"Look at you, girl! You're sex-ay."

Olivia laughed. "I don't know what's going on Mand. I'm not feeling like me . . . but I'm okay with that."

Mandie paused and looked at her friend. "You know, you look different . . . it's not just the hair. You have a glow about you... wait, are you wearing makeup?"

Olivia touched her face and nodded with a smile.

"Yeah . . . a little."

"You mean to tell me you pulled out your *special occasion mascara* to come to work today?"

"Yep."

"That's fucked up, man."

"That's not all," Olivia smiled. "I broke it off with Andrew, yesterday. He proposed to me in the park on the way back from Dr. Sketchy's, and I said 'No.' "

"Well, what do you know. Free at last!" Mandie yelled, raising her arms to the air. "Praise the Lord."

"But, wait . . . there's more. Yesterday morning when I opened the shop, I saw this sort of hot surfer guy out front and I brought him cupcakes. It's weird, I just wanted him right then and there out on the street."

"Did you do him?" Mandie asked.

"No!" Her face became flushed. "But, I sort of wanted to."

Mandie laughed, walked over and gave her friend a big hug, then placed her hands on Olivia's two cheeks, squeezing them together. In a maternal tone she said, "My little girl is growing up."

"I'm having fun, Mand."

"Good. You deserve it. Free from Mr. Rogers and his un-scuffed sneakers."

"Hey! I liked his sneakers!" Olivia said, laughing as she headed to the front to wipe down the display case.

On most days around one o'clock, Olivia went on break, leaving the bakery and walking down to go to her favorite chocolate shop in town, Ike's Confections. There she'd purchase a single cashew cluster as lunch. *Eighty-eight calories*—she had once calculated—after splitting it in half, of course. Food made so much sense when she divided it by twos . . . at least it had the day before.

Adella, the shop's owner, knew Olivia well. In fact, her daily visit was so predictable that Adella usually had the chocolate bagged up in crisp wax paper before she arrived.

The day before, Olivia had been so focused on maintaining her little routine that she had barely glanced at the sweets in the window, but today it was different. Today it felt as if the chocolate fudge spoke to her, begging her to come in.

"Hello, Adella," Olivia sang as she stepped in the store.

The older woman smiled big upon seeing Olivia.

"My goodness. I almost didn't recognize you. Look at you . . . a blond! That's a good color for you."

"Thank you," Olivia said cheerfully.

"You're early today. Give me a second and I'll bag it up."

"No, no. Wait. I think I need something different . . ." she said, inspecting the case.

"Really?" Adella laughed. "Well, I always say change is good."

"Yes, it is," Olivia said with a spirited smile. "Now, let me see . . ."

She peered through the glass.

Just thinking about the chocolate caused a rush of endorphins to course through her body. She pointed to something labeled Kahlua Seduction.

"One of those?" Adella asked.

"No . . . how about ten?" she laughed. "And give me two pounds . . . no, no . . . *three* pounds of the peanut butter fudge, and fifteen of the maple crèmes . . . and eleven of the turtles."

Adella peered at her over her glasses.

"You planning on sharing this with Miss Mandie?" she asked.

"Oh, I guess I hadn't thought of that. But, sure, that would be nice. Why don't you give me a pound of the licorice twists, then, too."

"No longer observing your special little diet?" Adella asked.

"You know, it just doesn't seem all that important anymore. New Olivia isn't going to be quite so stringent."

"Well, all right then, *New Olivia*."

Adella weighed the candy then walked to the cash register. As she rang up the order, Olivia played with a pinwheel resting on a shelf.

"Life is good, you know that, Adella?"

Adella gave her a look.

"Olivia, if I didn't know any better I'd think you were in love or something. I've never seen you so impulsive."

Olivia laughed and then paused to reflect on Adella's comment.

No one had ever called her impulsive before . . . or for that matter mistaken her for being in love. Flighty was for distractible women, with their heads in the clouds, not Olivia Parker the no-nonsense, pragmatic girl she was just yesterday.

"I'm definitely not in love, Adella." She paused, staring into a case. "But, I'm about to fall head over heels for the dark fudge in front of me."

She looked at Adella. "How about two pounds?"

"Can do," Adella nodded.

"Adella, I don't know what's gotten into me, but it's all good . . . I think."

"Well I'm happy you're happy; but just remember it is possible to have too much of a good thing," she said while lifting the heavy bag of candy and dramatically grunting. "That'll be seventy-three dollars and forty-six cents."

Olivia handed her a credit card and reached for the twelve-pound bag, amused at the astronomical price she would be paying.

"Thank you, my friend. Have a great day!" Olivia grinned and headed for the door.

Stepping onto the street, her hands instantly dug into the bag. She pulled out a box of fudge and opened it.

Feeling a wild hunger, she grabbed the thin plastic knife Adella had included in the bag and attempted to slice off a piece, but her ferocity was too intense and the knife broke in two.

Frustrated, she lifted the whole block to her mouth and sank her teeth in like it was a goliath chocolate bar. The sweet, the bitter, the saltiness instantly melted, not just onto her tongue, but into her being.

Feeling weak, her legs themselves like wilting licorice strands, she leaned herself against the wall.

Though she was now feeling lightheaded, nothing could stop her hunger.

She looked at the chocolaty mass and bit again, letting the dark taste roll over her tongue. Olivia took a few more bites and felt her body budding with pleasure. The street, the bustle of tourists dissolved away as she became conscious only of the chocolate that slid down her throat.

A few more bites and she found herself rising to her tip toes, her feet raising her up as she reached an unexpected height of ecstasy, alive with volcanic intensity.

"Oh, my God," she said, holding on to the wall for support, but just as she spoke someone interrupted her.

"It's that good, huh?" a man asked.

She opened her eyes and saw a familiar man in a worn leather vest and a t-shirt looking at her with a curious smile. She gave him a prolonged glance, and recognition set in.

"Well, hello there, stranger," she said with a doped-up grin, taking yet another bite of the fudge.

It took Brad a moment to realize who he was talking to as well. This creature was bright and wildly playful, a far cry from the girl on Wednesday, who had looked burdened with life.

"Hey there," he said, a brightness in his smile.

"I've never had fudge this good," she said as a smooth, content smile slipped across her face.

Brad laughed. "Yeah, I can tell,"

"Oh, where are my manners?" she laughed." Want some?" Olivia handed him the whole block complete with teeth marks gouged into it.

"Hmm. Tempting, but, no thanks. Though you're of course welcome to sit in front of my shop anytime and eat *all* the fudge you want. It might be good for business," he said grinning in amusement, the dark, seasoned lines crinkling around his eyes.

His hair was unkempt and slightly receding and just long enough to brush his shoulders. He had a worn, tired look, that suggested a hard life, but this look of fatigue was offset by the air of wit and wisdom that made him look young. His happy brown eyes and his jovial smile suggested to Olivia that perhaps life was just a series of good jokes to him.

Brad watched as she negotiated the melting fudge, licking her fingers one at a time. He felt himself drawn to her sweet awkwardness, her raw honesty. It was difficult for him to withhold the urge to move forward and ever so gently kiss her chocolaty lips.

He never went for the scrawny, collegiate types. He knew their kind. Sexually repressed, living off their daddy's money, out of touch with reality, yet here he was on Saint George Street feeling the strange urge to just lean himself against the building beside her and waste the day away.

The echo of laughter returned, and Brad turned his head in the direction of the sound. The shadow moved towards them.

"You see that?" he asked.

"Yes. I saw it follow you on your bike, the night of the accident," the once-mousy girl said, placing the remaining fudge back in its box.

Brad envisioned the dark creature trailing him all the way to the hospital and shuddered.

Olivia looked at him and said quietly, "Things have been so strange . . ." Her voice trailed off.

"Well, whatever it is. It's nothing to worry about. They say Saint Augustine is full of ghosts."

"Yeah, the only thing is, I don't think this is a ghost." She looked at him with a frown.

"Don't worry. Whatever it is, it can't hurt us," he answered with a tone that betrayed his confidence.

He looked at Olivia. The color had left her face. She was once again vulnerable, like she had appeared on Wednesday night.

He looked at her soft, sad features and felt the desire to console her, but he shook himself free from this thought. He needed to get back to work. The truth was he had no interest in soothing this woman's anxieties when he was working so hard to deny his own.

"Well, nice seeing you again. Have a good day," he said as he stepped into his store.

"Yeah . . ." Olivia answered, wrapping up the chocolate and placing it back in the bag.

Chapter 16

St. Augustine, Florida

October 8, 1969

Margret Johnson stared into the pan of eggs, one hand on the handle, the other one holding a spatula. She watched, detached, as breakfast turned from yellow, to brown, to black.

From the transistor on the kitchen table, a newscaster's staccato voice reported the week's body count—first for the Americans then the Viet Cong—then without even a pause The Archies were singing Sugar, Sugar.

Margret didn't hear any of it.

"Mom . . . Mom," a small voice said in the back of Margret's mind, like a neighbor's dog barking incessantly through the night.

She felt a tug on her sleeve.

"Mom." She heard it again and noticed Eliza at her side, looking angered.

"You're burning the eggs."

Margret blinked, suddenly conscious of the charred pan.

"What's wrong with you, Mom? Are you sick?"

"It's nothing. Mommy's fine. I just didn't sleep well."

"Isn't it time to go?"

Margret looked at the clock. "Yes, it is. I'm sorry." She turned off the burner and ran water over the black-encrusted eggs.

"Grab your bookbags."

"But mom, we haven't had breakfast," Bobby said from the kitchen table, a fork in hand. "I'm starving to death!"

Margret grabbed two slices of white bread and attempted to spread cold butter on them.

The bread stuck and curled into itself. She dropped it on Bobby's plate.

"Yuck. It's lumpy," Bobby said.

"I'm sorry, honey," Margret said, flustered.

Several nights earlier she had gone with her husband, Roger, out to L'Escargot Restaurant. It was an apology dinner. Roger was making up for his absence. Late nights at bars with "co-workers" had become a pattern, and he knew it was making Margret mad.

His apologies usually included a gift of some sort and, even though Margret could never let go of her hidden resentment, she always forgave him and now had his transgressions to thank for a jewelry box brimming with bracelets and necklaces.

But, last night, over two glasses of chardonnay, Margret received, not jewelry, but an antique box, hand carved with elaborate ferns and flowers.

Margret opened the box to find nothing inside—just a worn velvet liner. To her, diamond earrings would have been a much better choice, but she had to take what she could get.

The restaurant that night was crowded and seemed to Margret to be filled with many other husbands taking their wives out for apology dinners. She wondered if the woman sitting across from them would be getting jewelry.

Amid the din of the restaurant, she heard a woman's boisterous laughter—the voice of someone playfully amused. Margret looked around, curious to see which woman was actually having fun on her evening out. None fit the bill. She did, however, notice one woman who was sitting by herself, not laughing, engaged in nothing more than the bowl of lobster bisque in front of her. She looked content, in spite of being all alone with her soup, like she wouldn't rather be any other place but there.

Her long nose gave her a distinguished air, an older Nancy Sinatra perhaps, her blond hair piled on top of her head in an elegant bouffant. The woman looked up at her and smiled softly, and Margret had the desire to be there with this stylish woman, at her table, talking about Shakespeare or Moliere, rather than with Roger, who was currently recounting his golf game with *excruciating detail. It took all her might to stay in her chair and not go over to introduce herself.*

That evening after arriving back home, though Margret hadn't fully forgiven Roger, she was feeling friskier than she had in years. To Roger's delight, she was feeling so wild, in fact, that she chose to ride on top of him for their evening soiree. Perched over her husband, she found herself thinking not of him, but of the woman at L'Escargot. Although she tried to push the thought away, her building pleasure possessed her. At the height of ecstasy, a lively laughter filled the room and she felt herself peak like never before.

That next morning, she was not herself. Drained and distracted, she felt as if she wasn't even there as her children got ready for school. As they headed out the front door, through the window she saw her neighbor, Lydia, walking with her daughter across the street towards them.

As the kids ran to greet their neighbor friend, Margret froze in fear. Standing near Lydia was a silvery silhouette, a full, standing shadow, its dark body matching the cloudy sky. She closed and opened her eyes, hoping it would disappear, but it didn't. Lydia and the kids were oblivious to it.

Could this be a demon sent from hell to punish me for last night? *she wondered.*

Margret knew all about demons from her priest. It was Father Michael's favorite sermon topic. Demons never failed to grab his congregation's attention.

"Evil lurks all about in this world," he'd say. "Servants of Satan are watching you, waiting to pull you down."

Every time he talked about them, Margret got the chills. Roger scoffed at these lectures, arguing that it was Father

Michael's way of keeping his congregation in line. This infuriated her to no end.

"Your blasphemy will send you to hell," she had told her husband once. He had just laughed. Needless to say, Margret had prayed for her husband's soul more times than he deserved.

Margret patted her stiffly sprayed hair and assured herself she was fine. It was just the flu coming on, a fever-induced hallucination. But, regardless of how much she tried to convince herself, the shadow stayed and like Mary's little lamb it followed them to school.

Still oblivious to the creature, the kids ran ahead, their bookbags swinging wildly as they played a game of chase.

The shadow stayed close by, floating beside Lydia, forcing Margret to look at it as she listened to Lydia ramble.

"I went to the grocery store yesterday, and you know who had taken up residency in our very own plaza?"

"Who?" Margret asked, only half focused on her friend.

"Hippies. Hundreds of them."

"Why are they there?"

"I don't know. Probably to have their mass orgies—Oh!" she interrupted herself. "You're not going to believe what I heard. You know that Janis Joplin singer, the one who was on Dick Cavett last year?"

Margret barely heard her friend; instead, she looked almost through her. Margret's eyes focused on the creature now by Lydia's side.

When Margret didn't respond, Lydia just kept talking, "Oh, you know who I mean. That horrible hippie girl, with those feathers in her hair, who sounds like a colored woman when she sings?"

Lydia, in her yellow gingham dress, her perfectly applied eye liner, her peachy frosted lipstick, awaited a response. Margret just looked at her. She always thought her neighbor looked like a snapshot from Vogue Magazine.

Margret, on the other hand, was "a tad meaty," as her mother always said. "A little cheer in the rear." She knew she was not fat but still looked at pictures of Twiggy longingly, wishing her collar bone would jut out just a bit, like lovely Lydia's.

Margret nodded reflexively when she realized her friend was still talking.

"Well...I suppose this will come as no surprise, but . . ." she paused and whispered, "Janis Joplin sleeps with women."

Margret blinked at her in shock.

"I know. Jesus forgive her soul . . ." Lydia crossed herself. "And to think she could be influencing our children. Disgusting."

Lydia looked around to make sure no one was looking, then spoke, her nose turned up in revulsion. "I mean, what do they do, anyway? . . . you know . . ." Lydia said. ". . . without the proper parts?"

Margret heard the laughter from the previous night return, and she stopped suddenly as the world wobbled and warped. Oblivious to anyone around her, she froze, trapped in her own daydream.

In vivid detail she saw two young women in what appeared to be a New York flat, with large, abstract paintings hanging on the walls. Miles Davis was playing on a record player as the women sat beside each other on a mattress on the floor. They were touching each other in a way that Margret never imagined women would do. Yet Margret watched, in her dream, feeling almost as if she were there, experiencing a surprising amount of pleasure as the dark haired one leaned forward and placed her lips on the other girl's mouth.

"Margret?" Lydia called." Hello?"

She blinked and shook away the profane image. And to her surprise was standing with her kids at the front door of the school.

"Bye, Mom," Eliza and Bobby said.

Margret felt a sickening guilt in her gut, bile rising in her throat. What dark soul was taking her over?

As Lydia and Margret turned and headed back towards their homes, Lydia continued her rambling.

"So, please tell me you're going to Claudette's house for the Junior League meeting at one. I can't bear to be with that woman without moral support."

Margret barely heard her friend.

"Margret? What are you looking at?" Lydia asked, following her friend's line of sight.

"Nothing . . ."

"You don't look good, sugar," Lydia said. She reached into her purse." Here, you need one of these. Take one of my little blue pills?"

"Oh—no, no. I'm fine. I just need some rest."

"So, no Junior League?"

"I'm afraid not."

"Oh, poo," Lydia frowned.

"Lydia, I need to go," she said, feeling as if the trees were twisting and distorting in some sort of psychic hurricane.

"Okay. Take care, honey."

Margret stepped inside, leaned herself against the foyer wall, and looked up to the ceiling.

"Dear Jesus in Heaven, grant me the strength to overcome whatever dark creatures Satan has bestowed upon me."

She heard the laugh again, but this time it felt more maniacal. Holding herself up on the wall, Margret grabbed her purse and headed out the door.

The Johnsons' home was on Water Street, directly on the Matanzas River and just five blocks from the Cathedral Basilica, an easy walk on a September day. As she moved at a fast pace towards King Street, the recently renovated steeple with its Latin cross came into view.

Margret climbed the stairs and entered the nave. Grand arches, marble floors, and golden statues surrounded her as she turned to her right and knocked on the priest's office door.

Father Michael, the senior priest, answered. *"Why, hello, Mrs. Johnson."*

"I'm so sorry to bother you, Father."

"Oh, no bother. That's what I'm here for. Come in."

Father Michael gestured her into the office, which was lined on all sides with wooden bookshelves.

"Have a seat," he said, and she settled into a chair that sank down almost below his large antique desk.

"So, what seems to be your concern today?" he asked.

She took a deep breath.

"I know this sounds crazy, but . . . I think I'm being followed by a demon."

"Oh . . ." there was a pause. "Okay," he said. "I'm sorry to hear that."

Margret frowned.

"So you believe you're seeing demons?" the Father reiterated.

"Just one demon, actually," she said, now noticing the shadow as it hovered by a life-size statue of the Virgin Mary.

"And . . . I'm having . . . impure thoughts."

"Oh, really?" he asked

The creature laughed, and Margret once again felt herself slipping away, as if the demon's evil presence might cause her to melt right out of her seat into a puddle of nothingness on the marble floors. She forced her next words out.

"I'm having thoughts about . . ." she paused, then whispered, "sex."

"Is that so?" He asked.

"Yes . . ." She looked at the floor as she spoke. *"Sex with women."*

The shadow laughed, and Margret felt her heart pound.

The shadow climbed its way to the top of the statue, perched atop the Virgin Mary's head, and leaned forward from its roost like a gothic gargoyle, apparently entertained by Margret's predicament.

"Yes, well . . ." Father Michael cleared his throat. *"Satan's influence is everywhere. Even I am not immune to his ways."* He shifted again. *"These days, with the youth and their drugs and 'free love' in the media, it's becoming harder and harder to avoid Lucifer's power."*

Margret nodded.

"But to say you are being possessed by a demon is quite a stretch. In spite of my sermons, I must say demon possession is rare." He cleared his throat. *"With all due respect, my guess is you are just a bored housewife, in need of fanciful distractions. Hysteria, perhaps. But demonic possession is doubtful. In difficult times, I tell women like yourself to call upon Mother Mary to lead you on the true path to righteousness. She will show you the way."*

The laughter mocked the priest's words.

Margret found herself rising out of her chair, feeling suddenly like there was somewhere much more important to be.

Her eyes glassy, she spoke, "You are right, Father. It must be just a case of housewife boredom. Thank you for your time." *She excused herself and left the church.*

On the street the sun glared intensely, blinding Margret temporarily. She pulled out her sunglasses from her purse and stepped onto King Street.

Across the street from the Cathedral Basilica was the Plaza de la Constitución. The hot summer weather had finally broken, and people were milling about the town square. Music came from the center of the park where a group of thirty young people were sitting about on blankets, relaxing in the September sun. A man with a guitar sat near the center strumming a song she did not recognize, while nearby a barefoot woman spun, her long skirt ballooning out as she danced to a tune that only she heard.

Laughter came from the trees, and Margret looked up to see the shadow hanging up high in one of the oaks, like an irreverent monkey taunting her from above.

"No! You will not control me!" She shouted out loud at the impish being.

Several of the revelers turned and looked at this well-tailored woman speaking to the trees.

"You okay, lady?" one of the hippies called to her.

Doing whatever she could to fight the call of the revelers, her chest rose and she shouted,

"Heathens! You will not sway me!"

A few minglers began to chuckle.

Margret felt herself swell, her body light and tingly. And in that moment Margret Johnson of 1355 Water Street felt her ego, her sense of self, melt into the sidewalk into a heap of lost identity. Somewhere in the distance she heard the voices of concerned people rushing towards her, but she was already gone.

Margret woke, her head on a pillow, her body covered by a soft, worn quilt that smelled of exotic spices. A warm hand rested on her back, and she opened her eyes to see a young woman with fine, blond hair, deep blue eyes, and a light blue shawl wrapped around her shoulders.

"You took quite a fall, mama," she said, her voice delicate and angelic. "You feeling okay, now?"

Margret nodded, noticing that the sunlight from the open windows created an aura of golden radiance around the young woman's head.

"I'm Mary," the woman said.

Margret's eyes filled with tears.

"Oh, Mother Mary, I am sorry I failed you."

Mary laughed. "You didn't fail me, sister, and I ain't no mother. We all have a bad trip once in a while. Life's full of 'em; it's all just in how you handle them. What did you take, anyhow?"

"I didn't take anything," she said, humbled as Mary's blue eyes looked into her own.

Margret heard a voice from the other side of the room. "Hey, Mary, check her for concussion."

Margret turned to see a topless girl rolling a joint on a bedroom bureau. The shadow stood beside her.

Margret looked around and for the first time noticed her surroundings. She was in some sort of apartment. Discordant jazz played in the background while a man with a thin beard stood in the kitchen, making himself a sandwich.

"She's fine, April," Mary said, brushing a hand through Margret's hair. Mary walked to the other end of the bed by the topless girl and put her arm around her.

OPEN SOULS

"You feeling well enough to join us, mama?" Mary asked, taking the joint from April and taking a toke. Mary handed it back, eyeing April's breasts. She reached out and began gently tracing the girl's nipple. The two women climbed onto the bed beside Margret.

The topless girl leaned in and began kissing Mary softly and Margret watched, captivated by the beauty of the situation.

It occurred to Margret, in that moment, that she had been here before. This was her dream. The artwork, the music, the women were all the same.

Margret was where she was supposed to be.

Mary looked Margret's way and reached out to her. The resounding laughter of the demon returned, and Margret, compelled by her own desire, reached back to Mary.

Chapter 17

All night long, thoughts about his sick friend circled Brad's mind like vultures on a never-ending trail of death. Now, the next morning as he headed to the shop, he felt heavy from sleep deprivation. Brad was generally good at distracting himself, keeping the bad thoughts at bay, but today it felt like the negativity was winning.

As he headed down Saint George on foot, a woman dressed in skimpy pirate garb and handing out fliers for a pirate ship tour waved at him. She had been stationed at this spot for about four months and was becoming a nice fixture on Brad's morning walks to the shop. She had thick, luscious lips and a great ass that looked fantastic in her jagged-cut pirate skirt. He had planned to ask her out, but on this day all he could muster was a weary smile.

"Hey!" she called, waving a handful of fliers at him.

He nodded and moved on, focused on the road in front of him.

Brad glanced up and noticed overhead, on a porch cantilevered above the street, a billow of smoke that seemed to hover beneath the veranda. He paused to focus on it, wondering if Sangria's Wine Bar was on fire, but then he realized this smoke had shape to it, character, suggesting the silhouette of a man casually leaning over the rail, comfortably watching the afternoon bustle. A low, demonic chuckle rumbled down the street.

His heart quickening, Brad looked around him. Vacationers continued moving down the block in their typical tourist daze, unaware of Brad's vision. The creature looked down at him then shifted an arm as if raising a glass in a toast to poor Brad on the street. It laughed again.

Wanting to be as far away from the creature as he could, Brad picked up his pace, moving with a large stride until he was blocked by a group of distracted tourists standing in the middle of the street.

"I think we should eat at the place we ate at last year . . . you know, the one with the neat water wheel," one woman said, her jewelry jangling as she negotiated the bulging shopping bags in her hands.

"No, Gertie. We did that last year. Their fish sandwich was just so-so. How about this Mi Casa place?"

"Hey! Are you a local?" Brad heard a woman calling loudly at him, and she grabbed his arm.

Brad gritted his teeth. Tourists were a blessing and a curse for him. Even on days when he felt their presence irritating, he was always kind. They were the life blood of his tattoo business, though these two would certainly not be visiting his place.

"Yeah, I live here," he said looking back for the shadow.

"Can you tell us where to eat? What's good?"

"Mi Casa is a good bet." He said his eyes still fixed down the narrow street where the shadow was heading towards him.

"Thank you, dear," the woman said with a thick New Jersey accent.

Brad gave them a nod and picked up speed again only to be blocked a few yards later by two little boys flashing their brand new pirate swords in a mock battle.

The shadow hovered just yards away, its darkness an aberration in the bright Florida sun. Brad stood dead center in the street, absolutely still, and the laughter began again.

The crowd appeared to waver and melt, and Brad's mind moved more slowly as he found himself no longer there on the street but now in the Iowa of his childhood.

He was nine, his brother Jerry twelve. They were standing in front of their small family bungalow surrounded by rows of corn. The boys were using the long branches of a weeping willow as swords, whapping each other's thighs, causing bright red marks on their legs. Brad yelped and jumped, laughing the whole time, until his mother came out.

Brad could see her with crisp acuity—her smooth skin, her bright eyes, her pearly lip gloss. He swore he could even smell her perfume. On this day she wore a pink mini dress with white and yellow daisies, her hair long and straight, hanging past her shoulders.

Completely lost in the dream, fifty-one-year-old Brad sat himself down in the middle of Saint George Street, unaware of the movement of bodies around him.

"*Cut that out, you two,*" he heard his mother say. "*You're going to make each other bleed.*"

"*That's the point,*" Brad snickered.

"*Look at your legs!*" *she said as she pointed to Brad's thigh. Young Brad paused to check out his war wounds, when his brother whapped him on the behind. Brad turned to retaliate.*

Brad's mother rolled her eyes and bent down to check her lipstick in the side mirror of his dad's freshly waxed Chevy.

"*Dad and I are going out. There's TV dinners in the freezer.*"

As she spoke, his dad, in a nicely pressed, bell-bottomed suit, stepped out of the house, the screen door slamming behind him.

"You and your God damned hair and makeup, Grace. We're already fifteen minutes late."

Brad watched his dad place his hand around the back of his mother's neck as if guiding her to the car. This action could have passed for affection to some, but Brad knew it was more an attempt to steer her, keep her under control.

His dad turned to the boys and said, "You think you retards can handle us being gone until midnight?"

The boys nodded solemnly.

He pointed his finger directly and them and said, "We're trusting you. Don't fuck up."

Brad and his brother, Jerry, who were both never comfortable with to their father's abrasiveness, nodded. Brad watched the car roll off.

The dream dissolved, bringing him back to the present in Florida. There he was, his shoulders knotted, sitting right in the middle of Saint George. People passed him on either side, giving the heavily tattooed biker a large span of space, but Brad did not feel embarrassed. He did not feel shame. All he felt was lingering rage.

Shaken from his vision, Brad felt as if he had just wakened from a fitful night's sleep. Trying to get his bearings, he stood and looked around. Ignoring the gawking looks as he went, he hauled his body towards the shop.

Brad paused at Ike's Confections and stared at a row of caramel apples, lined up like soldiers awaiting the onslaught of snack-time tourists. His mom used to get him caramel apples when she'd take him to the circus each summer. Just the smell alone of the warm sugar wafting from the store was enough to bring a little smile to his face. He walked a few blocks south and approached Phoenix Tattoo.

The booming sound of death metal poured out onto the street, and as he got closer he realized it was coming from his store. The front door was wide open, letting the air conditioned air onto the hot street.

He felt his rage swell as he entered the shop to find a female customer in chaps and a tight, fringed leather vest lying on the couch. She looked up from her copy of Easy Rider magazine and smiled at him.

At Brad's station, Buzz sat, tattoo machine in his hand, the sound of its vibrant hum filling the store. An open bottle of Wild Turkey sat on the counter near Buzz's workspace. Ink bottles were spread haphazardly, and dirty needles lay discarded like a game of pick-up sticks on the counter.

"What the fuck?" Brad yelled, storming across the shop and turning off the music. "What the hell are you doing here?"

"Oh, hey, man . . . actually I came by with a few friends after the shop closed last night. They wanted some ink done. Been here tattooing all night. Right, Felicity?" Buzz said, looking to the girl with the magazine.

"That's right," she smiled as she chewed her gum.

The woman Buzz was working on laid on her belly on a padded table as he etched a warped Betty Boop into her skin. Just looking at it made Brad cringe.

Brad tapped the poor woman on the shoulder. "I need to talk to Buzz for a moment. We'll be right back."

Buzz put down the tattoo machine and gave Brad a confused look, as if he had no idea what could possibly be fueling Brad's rage.

The men entered the stockroom and Brad shut the door behind them. Breathing short breaths, he looked Buzz straight in the eye, suppressing the immediate desire to beat him to a pulp.

"What the hell makes you think you can take over my shop like it's some sort of seedy night club, then tattoo clients you don't have permission to handle? Maybe you don't remember, but you're still in training. You go by my rules." Brad knew the customers could hear every word he said, but he didn't care.

He continued listing Buzz's violations: "So you think it's okay to drink in my shop, mistreat supplies, take new customers without my approval . . . not to mention stay open all fucking night!"

"Whoa there, old man. I was helping you out. Where's the gratitude?"

Ready to smack him, Brad swallowed hard. Just as he was about to begin a string of cusswords, he noticed the dark shadow slide its way through the wall into the room. The creature greeted him with a chuckle. Brad froze.

As the dark being's laughter intensified in growing amusement, Brad felt his rage leave him. His fury was replaced with something worse—unbearable sadness. He felt the despair move through his body like a dark fog as he began to ache with longing and despair.

The shadow remained in its spot, watching, as if reveling in Brad's upheaval.

Buzz looked from his boss to the empty space where Brad stared. Confused, he asked, "So . . . what? We good, man?"

Brad felt the muscles in his shoulder blades tighten even more, his eyes stinging with budding tears. He placed his hands over his face as if this action could halt the onslaught of sorrow, but the sobs began to come. He lowered himself onto a stockroom box, crippled by his new emotions.

Buzz looked at his boss, puzzled.

"Really?" Buzz said, and he slinked to his station to clean up.

The shadow now brought itself over to a stack of boxes beside Brad and settled down, reclining back as if completely satisfied with its job. It seemed to Brad as if its plan was to torment him until he was nothing more than a puddle of sorrow on the floor.

"If you're death coming for me, I can take it," he said. "Just stop with the agony. No more chaos." And with his words, without explanation, the creature rose and faded into the stockroom walls.

Brad took a deep breath.

"What the fuck is happening to me?" he muttered to himself. He then stood up, wiped his eyes, cleared his throat, and headed to the front room.

The girl who had been waiting had gone, leaving the one woman alone on the table, bare back exposed to the room, her pathetic Betty Boop awaiting repair. When Brad entered, Buzz was re-dipping his gun and beginning to color the cartoon character's hair.

Normally Brad would have just fired the idiot, but he was afraid to make a move, afraid of what flood of emotions would come out if he were to speak. Any more conflict and he was liable to kill the asshole.

The girl being tattooed turned her head, looked to Buzz, and said, "Hey, you told me this was your studio. Whose place is this really?"

Holding his position, Brad spoke. "Buzz, you're done."

Buzz tossed the gun onto the counter and muttered under his breath, "I could run this shit hole better than you." He grabbed his keys and his cigarettes and went out the door.

Relieved to have the douche bag gone, Brad returned to the girl.

"You good down there?" Brad said, speaking to the torso below him.

"Uh huh. How's it look?" she asked nervously. She smelled of alcohol too. Apparently she had been partaking in Buzz's Wild Turkey, too.

Brad looked at the train wreck of a tattoo before him and mustered up the best lie he could.

"It looks nice. Real nice. Is it okay if I finish this for you?"

"Okay," the girl spoke. "But, can you keep the style the same?"

"Sure," he answered, knowing regrettably that Buzz's "style" was that of a drunken monkey. He dipped the gun into the black ink and did his best at mending the irreparable mess, though he knew with tattoos—and life—there was no going back, no fixing what had already been done.

Chapter 18

When Mandie finally returned from her break Sunday afternoon, Olivia thought she was going mad. She needed to get out of that eight-hundred-square-foot shop, be part of the open air, and absorb the living energy of her town.

After a brief exchange with Mandie, Olivia left the shop on her break, entering the action of the street. As she moved down Saint George, Olivia felt like Dorothy skipping down the yellow brick road, keeping a slight hop in her step. To Olivia it was like someone had repainted the world in day-glow intensity, the normally dull street humming with magical joy.

Up ahead, in a crowd of silver-headed retirees, she spied the shadow. But, the closer she got the farther away it moved, pushing forward as if it had some sort of agenda.

OPEN SOULS

The shadow stopped at the foot of the stairs of a shop Olivia knew well. Judas Priest sang loud from the doorway of The Cat's Meow. Other days it was Black Sabbath or Motorhead—never music to her liking, but today the heavy vocals seemed potent and alive.

The Cat's Meow had been in business for several years and was filled with studded leather jackets, biker vests, and t-shirts. Beside the front counter was a collection of stickers and patches with crude slogans and obscenities. The store drew in bikers during Bike Week and Biketoberfest as well as tourists wanting a piece of the biker life.

Although Olivia wouldn't normally consider going to The Cat's Meow, on this afternoon she felt a desire to be part of the forbidden and unknown. So, following the shadow, Olivia approached the store, but as she placed her foot on the first step, her world began to sway and the four-hundred-year-old building seemed to give in to the demands of time, falling in on itself. She held tightly onto the railing, looking upward toward the open door from where the shadow watched her.

Ignoring her tilting world, she grasped the hand rail and continued up the stairs into the shop. She watched ahead as the shadow wandered through the store, in and out of the racks. In spite of her delirium, Olivia pursued it. Just as she reached the creature, the walls closed in on her and it seemed as if dark ink seeped across her vision. Olivia felt herself melt to the ground and everything went black.

When she woke, the world had once again stabilized and her head no longer swooned. She blinked her eyes to focus and saw she was no longer in The Cat's Meow but instead right up against a large plate-glass window. On the other side, she could make out two people, their voices a soft mumble through the glass.

Inside, on the far end of the shop, a girl was lying face down on a table. Olivia could only see the man's back, wisps of grey hair curling out from beneath a black doo rag. He appeared to be in his element, relaxed and centered.

Olivia observed him with curiosity, unconcerned about the fact that her face was pushed smack dab against a shop window. She noted that there was a dark shape by the man's side; without a doubt, this was the shadow she had been seeing

The man wiped excess ink from the woman's back, looked at his handiwork, said something to the girl, and tossed his gloves into the garbage can. She stood and looked into a large mirror along the wall, smiled, and paid at the front desk. Olivia watched a few moments later as the woman stepped out into the street. She looked Olivia up and down with a critical eye then headed down Saint George.

Meanwhile, as the man inside tidied up his station, Olivia noticed the shadow moving to the window.

"Hey, lady!" a voice said from behind.

Olivia jumped. She turned around to see a lanky man she didn't recognize, a cigarette between his nail-bitten fingers.

He blew a puff of smoke upward. Olivia's eye followed the cloud as it dispersed into the afternoon sky.

"You don't look like you're from around here," he said with an accent that suggested he had moved from place to place during his life.

Olivia answered. "I'm from North Carolina, originally, but I live in town. Been here for almost ten years. I own the cupcake shop down the street," she said, gesturing down the way.

"Right on," he said, taking another drag. He brought a worn brown bag to his lips and then offered it to her.

"Wild Turkey?" he asked

"No, thank you," she said.

The man's eyes lingered on her breasts. He raised his eyebrows and took another swig.

No one ever looked at her breasts. There wasn't much to see. Mandie told her once that with the right bra, her tits could look great, but Olivia was perfectly fine with her JCPenny's sport bras.

Curious as to why this guy seemed so interested, she discreetly looked down and noticed she wasn't dressed in the clothes she had put on that morning. In place of her baggy t-shirt was a tight corset, pushing her breasts into two ripe peaches, more visible to the world than they'd ever been. On her legs were—of all things in the Florida heat—black leather chaps, with exceptionally short jean shorts underneath, embellished with silver studs. Her old clothes were nowhere to be seen.

The guy brought his arm towards her and reached to the back of her neck. She looked at him, sure he was trying to make a move, when she felt a tug on her corset

From behind her he pulled off a store tag that was apparently still on the clothes.

"Seventy bucks? Now that's some top," he said.

Suddenly becoming conscious of another tag at her waist line she reached down and pulled it off. This was for $110.

"So, you're a little thief? A bad girl, huh?" He snickered. "Though I have to tell you, if you're gonna wear stolen stuff, I highly suggest pulling the tags off, first."

Olivia had a faint memory of seeing this top and chaps on the rack at The Cat's Meow, but she had no recollection of trying them on let alone pulling them off the rack. She did, however, remember the sick swooning she had felt in the shop and it occurred to her that she might have very well blacked out. For all she knew, she could have stolen them.

As confusion and guilt percolated in Olivia's mind, a new sensation, spurred on by the laughter of her demon, took its place. This was not a feeling of shame, but of pleasure. Absolute thrill.

Almost reflexively she reached for the bottle of Wild Turkey and took a hefty swig, letting the alcohol bring fire to her insides.

She felt her whole body relax, and a seductive smile slipped across her face as she looked at the man, whose grin revealed a line of crooked, yellowed teeth. He was not attractive, not in the least, but in the moment it seemed like he might be a decent conquest.

"I'm Buzz," he said, sensing her shift in demeanor.

"Mmm. Nice to meet you, Buzz." She smiled with drowsy contentment, then right there on the open street; she leaned in and gave this man, whose breath smelled of Wild Turkey and Cool Ranch Doritos, a slow kiss on the lips.

She pulled away, a grin across her face, and tilted her head back, revealing the soft bare skin of her neck. She spoke slow and sultry.

"How strange my life has become."

"Strange for sure," Buzz nodded, then as if remembering some far off responsibility he was failing to do he said, "Man, I gotta get going, but give me your phone," he said.

In her daze, she handed it over.

He entered his number and then, under the space for his name, he wrote:

For a good time call.

Then, he brought himself once again towards her, his cloud of stale cigarette smoke moving with him, and laid his mouth to hers.

As his tongue wrapped around hers the door to the tattoo shop opened, and the man Olivia had been watching stepped out, the shadow trailing behind him like a faithful pet.

Upon seeing Brad, Buzz pulled away from Olivia as if he were a teenager caught with a girl in his bedroom.

"Oh, hey," Buzz said concealing his erection with the brown bagged whiskey.

"Fun's over," Brad said, his voice infused with anger. "Time to go home, Buzz."

"You've got my number," Buzz said to Olivia before heading down the street. He mouthed the words "Call me."

Brad stepped from the shop door into the street.

"How do you know Buzz?" he asked.

"I don't know him at all," she paused." I just met him . . . seems nice."

"Yeah, well, looks can be deceiving."

The ghostly laughter started again and Brad looked at Olivia.

"You hear it?" she asked.

He nodded solemnly. "I'm hearing it everywhere."

She watched Brad closely as he leaned against the wall and folded his arms across his chest. The shadow mimicked him on the far side of the wall. Olivia somehow found this funny.

She sized Brad up. He was maybe fifteen years older than she. He had a weather worn look, leathered skin from too much sun and too many cigarettes, but there was something desirably masculine about him. Cocky and confident, he seemed unwilling—maybe unable—to falter from his cool-headed demeanor.

As she looked at the greying bristles on his chin, Olivia felt a warm desire building, reverberating throughout her body. While the thought of fucking Buzz was inspired by something outside herself, with Brad it was more like a growing heat, like her own internal embers fueled by someone's warm breath.

Brad produced a pack of Marlboros and offered her one. She looked at it hesitantly, paused, and then took one. She held it out awkwardly between her fingers . Aware of but unconcerned about her exposed breast line, she bent forward and gave him a smile as he offered her a light.

"So is this, like, your thing—hanging outside of tattoo shops?" He leaned back against the stucco wall and exhaled a puff of smoke. The shadow, mocking his movements did the same. Brad glanced at it briefly then looked away.

Olivia laughed. "No . . . though it's starting to look like that, huh? Ever since we found that box I've been doing things that just aren't me, like talking to that Buzz guy . . . and *this*," she said, gesturing to the cigarette. "I never went through the bad girl thing in my teens or in college, and frankly I never thought I would, but now I'm just feeling a lot more open," she said.

To Brad, even in her seductive clothing this girl seemed like a fledgling being, a newly hatched butterfly, her wings recently spread, waiting for the moment when they were dry enough to fly. He couldn't stop looking at her.

She eyed him back. Somehow his gruff "don't touch me" appearance didn't put her off in the least.

"You know," she continued, "it's like I've got a little devil on my shoulder who's getting me into all kinds of trouble."

He chuckled.

"So, you don't usually dress like a biker babe?" he asked.

"No. Never. I mean, chaps? Come on! I feel like friggin' catwoman."

"Well, I must say, the catwoman thing is working for you."

Olivia smiled.

"You know, I don't even have a single tattoo."

"Not one?" Brad mocked.

"Not one. Never wanted one."

"Well, I know a good guy, if you're ever in the market for one. I hear he's the best."

Olivia gave him a lingering smile.

"I can't believe I've told you all this . . . and here you saw me kissing some random guy."

"Yeah, well that random guy was my employee... *and* he's got a girlfriend. Just saying. Not to mention he's a royal asshole,"

"A girlfriend? Really? Well, crap."

A long moment lingered between them, and Olivia realized that if she didn't break the silence and start rambling she would uncontrollably wrap herself around this man and not let go.

"I just dumped my boyfriend, you know? He proposed to me the night you and I met." She blew out a stream of smoke, savoring the rush of air as it blew past her lips.

"Sex was awful with him." She tapped the ashes onto the ground.

"Shit! I'm sorry," she said. "This is what I'm talking about, about being more open. I don't normally go blurting out my personal life to strangers. Things are just so odd." She took a drag and started coughing uncontrollably.

The dark laughter returned and the two looked at each other with concern.

"What the hell is happening to me? I mean, what the *fuck*?" Olivia asked, satisfied with her word choice. "Just two days ago I was me, boring Olivia. Now I have no idea who I am. I feel like some sort of puppet, like my fate is being written as we speak . . . and somehow you are written into it, too."

She looked to Brad for a response, but he was changing to a whitish hue.

Brad was feeling light, as if his limbs were detached from his body, so open, so vulnerable that the soft breeze might blow him over. The shadow chuckled, teasing him with his own weakness. As the world swirled, he focused on the girl's lips. They drew him in like a foreign fruit, juicy and tantalizing, wanting to be tasted. He was overcome with the urge to bring her in close, not to fuck her but simply to be surrounded by her scent.

"My name's Olivia, by the way. I own the cupcake shop down the street," she said, reaching out her hand to shake his.

Brad smiled, stabilizing himself on the wall.

"Olivia, huh? You like olives?" he asked.

"Hate 'em," she said. "Makes me crazy when people think they're cute and call me Olive."

"Well then, it's a pleasure to meet you, *Liv,*" he said, feeling himself become steady.

"Oh, not Liv. That's what my annoying cousin used to call me."

"I dunno. It seems to suit you."

She smiled then looked away, causing an awkward pause to hang between the two of them. Brad broke the silence.

"Hey, I was planning on getting myself a caramel apple today. Why don't you let me get you one, too?"

She gave him a knowing smile. "Is this some sort of a biker-dude come on?"

"No. Really. Just an apple, that's all." Brad said.

"Well, all right then. And, for the record, caramel doesn't work on me like fudge—at least I don't think it does," she said.

"Well, like I said, I'm not trying to do anything. Scout's honor."

"You don't look like much of a boy scout," Olivia said with a sly grin, still intensely magnetized to this man.

"I was a boy scout for three years!"

"Really? What happened?" she teased.

"The Seventies happened."

"Sex, drugs, and rock and roll?"

A moment of sadness flashed across Brad's face, like he was remembering something he could never share, but as fast as the misery came it was gone.

"Give me a second. I'll be right back."

She watched as he slipped into the candy store next door and returned a few minutes later holding two softball-sized apples on sticks, with a grin on his face that made him look like he was nine years old.

He handed her one.

"You know, you haven't told me your name," she said, taking a blissful bite.

"Brad," he said as he watched her lick caramel from her lips.

"Nice to meet you, Brad."

"Well, *Liv*, it's good to meet you, too." He smiled as she took another bite. "You really do enjoy your food, don't you?" he asked.

She laughed out loud. "Actually, I hate it. Or two days ago I did, anyhow. Food makes me crazy. Except for now . . . I mean, you know that fudge, yesterday? It was better than sex."

"Really? Well then you're not having sex with the right men," Brad smiled. "Did you already eat *all* that chocolate you bought?" he asked.

"Almost," she giggled. "If this keeps up, I'm going to be the size of a whale by Christmas." With her free hand, she attempted an elegant drag of the cigarette, but broke out coughing again.

He smiled, amused by this oddity of a woman in front of him.

"You know," Brad said. "I've worked across from this candy shop for almost a decade. And, until this moment, I've never set foot in there. And here I am buying fucking caramel apples for some strange chick who just smoked her first cigarette."

"You can tell?" she said, awkwardly shifting the cigarette in her hand.

"You can't hide much from me."

"Well then, Mr. Mysterious Tattoo Man. I'll be sure to be careful around you."

She smiled and lifted the apple upward, suggesting a toast.

He raised his.

"To not knowing who the fuck we are!" he said.

"To not knowing who we are. Cheers!"

"Cheers," he said

And they both bit into their treats, letting the tart juice of the apples burst into their mouths, as their teeth filled with caramel sweetness—a perfect balance of sour and sweet, the flavors melted deep within their happy souls.

Chapter 19

Brad entered the shop with a huge grin on his face, a far departure from the mood he was in less than an hour ago. He moved around the Phoenix, humming to himself. In this moment his strange and shitty life felt almost manageable.

He walked over to toss the remaining apple core into the trash but stopped abruptly when he noticed the shadow move through the window into the shop. With Olivia around, the shadow's presence didn't seem quite so bad, but now alone, he felt powerless. Keeping his eye on the creature, he walked to the supply room, maintaining a safe distance. The shadow followed, gliding closer as its sinister laughter snaked its way into his brain. Once again, Brad felt the walls of the room warp and he found himself propelled back in time to a moment he had tried to forget.

He was in his boyhood home. His eleven-year old self casually sketched pictures while he sat on his bed —a knight confronting a looming dragon—when a loud thud echoed against the walls. The noise was followed by a panicked scream.

"You fucking bitch! I told you to stay away from him." His father's voice rattled the walls.

"I didn't do anything, I swear!" Brad's mom pleaded.

"You think I can't tell when you lie, you bitch? I saw you talking with him. Filthy cunt!"

There was a slap, skin on skin, a thud, followed by the sound of his mother sobbing and pleading with his dad.

"No. No more," she begged. "I didn't do anything. I didn't. I promise."

When a third slap was heard, young Brad had had enough. He rose from his bed and picked up the metal baseball ball bat resting in the corner of his room. With his fingers choked tight around the neck. Brad, a short-statured eleven-year-old, entered his parents' room. His mother was on the bed, folded over herself, bright red blood oozing from her head. His father, standing over her, looked at Brad with his snake eyes.

His dad's casual tone was a sharp contrast to the anger on his face. "Hey, Bradley. How are you?"

Brad stood his ground, his hands gripping the bat tightly, his chest rising up and down, ready to fight.

"*Your mom and I are just having a disagreement. We're fine. You can put the bat down.*"

"*Get out,*" Brad said in a growl.

"*Son, if you know what's good for you, you'll leave now.*"

"*No. Mom, come on.*"

He looked to her, her soft blond locks cascading on a pillow, but she didn't move.

"*Brad this is between your mom and me. Now, go on.*"

"*No. You're not going to hurt her anymore.*"

Brad cautiously stepped forward, but as he moved to take his mom's hand, his dad's arm came forward, yanked the bat away, tossed it aside and slapped Brad hard, knocking him to the ground. Everything went black.

Chapter 20

Brad returned to the present, forty years later, in the same position his dad had left him in, a broken child curled in defeat. In spite of decades passed, his face still stung, his heart burdened with helplessness and pain. But as Brad came to, he realized he was no longer in the shop. He was lying on a patch of grass in the cool of night.

In his peripheral vision, a row of sail boats and dinghies bobbed up and down silently with the quiet pulse of a dark river. The Bridge of Lions was to his left not even half a block away. It appeared that he was at the municipal marina not far from the Phoenix, but why or how he had gotten there was unclear. As he brought himself to sitting, he noticed he was dangling a dying cigarette, mostly ashes now, between two slightly singed fingers.

He rose and walked to the river's concrete edge and peered in. The water, silver from the moon, lapped like liquid mercury against the side. He glanced over to the stone lions that stood undeterred, and his mind went to Olivia.

A cacophony of laughter broke through his thoughts, and Brad in his weakened state felt a burning urge to do nothing more than strip off his clothes and jump into the water.

Brad didn't know anyone who swam in the brackish Matanzas River—unless they were really drunk and stupid. Stories of aggressive bull sharks and alligators pulling down large dogs circulated regularly through the community, but that didn't matter. For Brad, the sudden longing to be immersed in the darkness was unbearable.

He pulled off his t-shirt then reached down and removed his boots. Not bothering to scan the area for people, he unbuttoned his shorts and slid down his boxers, exposing himself completely. The thick Florida air blew hot across his shoulders.

Though he was aware at that moment of the absurdity of being stripped down to nothing in downtown Saint Augustine, his apprehension was overshadowed by the desire for release, liberation, a cleansing away of his pain. This was where he was meant to be, in the moment, completely free.

In his fresh, unfettered state he leaped out and plunged into the deep water, letting its liquid luminosity wrap around him, embracing him like a goddess with a thousand arms. He surfaced and exhaled in a call of conquest, feeling more alive than he had in years. He pulled back his wet hair, looked to the shore, and noticed someone standing at the edge watching him.

Chapter 21

After enjoying the caramel apple with Brad that afternoon, Olivia returned to Eat it Too. She had been gone far longer than her one-hour break, but Mandie didn't seem to mind. Mandie was thrilled that her friend was dressed in something more interesting than her regular *man* clothes.

"Honestly, Olivia, I never thought this would happen to you!"

"What?" Olivia asked.

"You finding yourself. Breaking out of that God damned shell."

"I don't know if I'd call this finding myself. I call it having fun."

"Exactly!" Mandie's eyes lit up. "In my book, letting yourself have fun *is* finding yourself!"

"I suppose." Olivia thought for a second. "So, what do you think? Does finding myself also involve feeling horny all the time? Because I'm feeling this odd energy towards men, like I never have before."

"I think you're tapping into your dark side, but not like your bad dark side. You've hit that part of you that you always kept down. You know, your id."

"Well then, I have to confess, my id has the hots for a fifty-one-year-old tattoo artist who rides a motorcycle."

Mandie laughed. "Yeah, I just can't see you with a biker . . . actually, you know maybe it's not your id doing this after all, maybe the hair dye messed with your brain cells."

Olivia laughed. "Have people ever gone mad from peroxide before?"

Mandie looked at her friend in the black bustier and smiled. "It's possible . . . Maybe you and Ms. Clairol need to have a talk."

Olivia smiled.

Mandie looked at Olivia for a long moment, as if afraid to bring something up.

"You know, O, since you're being so adventurous . . . trying new things and such . . . I was thinking . . . well . . . I know you're not into weed and all but . . ."

"Yes!" Olivia answered.

"But I didn't even finish."

"Yes, I want to smoke pot with you and Tank. I'd love to."

Olivia could hardly contain her excitement, so much so that she insisted they close the shop early. When they arrived at Mandie's place, Tank was already there, stoned and laughing to himself at videos of cats wedged into boxes on his laptop.

Olivia went in and sat right down on the living room floor, anxious for her night to begin, laughingly pulling Mandie down beside her. Though Olivia and Tank had never really bonded, when he saw her ready and rearing, he joined them on the floor, happy to see Olivia finally joining the fold.

Tank took a hit then passed the bong to Olivia. She wrapped her lips around the glass tube and inhaled deeply. The water in the vessel percolated with little pops, releasing puffs of smoke into her lungs. She removed her mouth and sealed her lips, waiting for the tightening in her chest to build until she couldn't hold it any longer. She exhaled, letting the smoke disperse, and then passed the glass tube to Mandie.

A few more hits and it seemed her mind was melding with the music on Mandie's iPod.

"The song is making my fingers come alive. I don't think they're part of me anymore," she said as she watched her fingers turn and twirl in some foreign dance.

"I just knew you'd be fun to get stoned with." Mandie grinned.

"I just knew I'd be fun to get stoned with, too," Olivia said, and she joined her friend in hysterics.

Tank looked at the women sitting in their respective bean bags and said, "Damn, you two are like sexy snakes or something, all smooth and long and shit."

"No, we're like the sexy cupcake snake charmers of Saint Augustine," Mandie said. She nodded toward her friend. "Tank, doesn't Olivia look hot with blond hair?"

"Oh, yeah…I think she's actually a mermaid that becomes human just long enough to screw pirates and smoke weed."

Olivia took a strand of her blond hair and gazed at it as she wrapped and unwrapped it around her finger.

"I've got mermaid hair. That's why I'm so powerful these days. The mermaid hair makes me beautiful and *tasty*."

Tank and Mandie both started laughing.

"Mmm, yummy Olivia," Mandie joked, and then interrupting herself she said, "Hey! You know what we should do?"

"What?" Olivia asked, excited.

"We should totally go down to the shop and make, like, some kind of masterful concoction."

"Oh, my God. Yes," said Olivia. "Like something out of caramel and pecans and cashews . . . that, like, oozes when you eat it. Then we can, like, hand it out to all the dessertless people in the world."

"Totally. We'll be the saints of Saint George Street," Mandie said. "God, you've been a blast lately, sister. What the heck happened to you? If it's not the hair dye, what is it? You doing crank or something?"

Olivia thought of the wooden box sitting safely at home on the kitchen table. Then, thinking herself the cleverest woman alive said, "Let's just say I'm no longer all *boxed* up inside... I've *opened* up!"

When Mandie and Olivia arrived at the shop, it was close to eleven o'clock. Still giddy, they let themselves in and headed for the kitchen where they measured and mixed.

"You know what? We should totally be stoned at the bakery *all* the time," Olivia said, proud of her brilliance.

"Honey, I've been stoned since I was fourteen years old," Mandie said.

"Of course you have." Olivia grinned, wondering to herself why she hadn't realized this fact before.

Olivia headed to the front room for more cupcake liners. As she dug around, she noticed a subtle movement out on the dark street. Wondering who would be at their door so late, she looked out and saw the shadow outside the window.

"Hi there!" she said to the creature, waving like a little girl to Santa Claus.

"Who you talking to?" Mandie called from the back room as she dipped her finger into the mixing bowl and pulled out a stray egg shell.

"My shadow. It watches me and makes me do weird shit," Olivia giggled.

The women baked cupcakes for several hours while the shadow, now inside the shop, watched them closely. Although the effects of the marijuana seemed to be lessening, Olivia still felt high.

When the cupcakes were frosted and decorated, Olivia heard Mandie say something to her about heading home, but whatever she said didn't reach Olivia's ears, which were now filled with the laughter of the shadow. Sounds and lights blurred together as the floor rippled, the walls melted, and solid thoughts dissipated like smoke. Olivia was lost to the moment.

Chapter 22

Time had passed, but she was not sure how much, nor did she have any idea what had happened since she last saw Mandie, but it didn't matter. Not one bit.

Olivia was now in front of the Bunnery Café, still on Saint George. There were no people around, so it had to be late. She guessed around two in the morning, but she really had no clue.

Her mind no longer felt warped by the drugs. In fact, she felt acutely aware of everything around her. Her skin was charged, as if the surrounding molecules were bouncing against her arms, laying kisses on her limbs. She no longer wore the chaps and shorts Buzz had found her in but, instead, had on the skirt she was originally wearing that morning.

Unconcerned about the holes in her memory, she kicked off her flip flops and abandoned them beside Kernel Poppers Popcorn Shop. She walked barefoot down the street, tuned into the sensation of her soles pressing against the heated pavement. She was there, alone in the darkness, enjoying the blissful moment, unconcerned about the past or the future.

The dance of bugs in a nearby street light was enough of a distraction to cause her to forget all about her friend, who she figured was still back up at the shop cleaning alone. None of it mattered. She inhaled the night air, more relaxed than she had felt in years. She was free of attachment, alive in the magic of the ancient city.

From a few yards ahead, the shadow watched her. Back at the shop, it had appeared to be close to Olivia's size—a small five-foot-something, but now it reached almost six feet high, its ghostly silhouette broader, more solid in form.

"Well, hello, sir, how do you do?" Olivia asked with a playful bow.

The shadow gave a rumbling laugh, and then as if Olivia no longer mattered, it glided down the street away from her, heading south towards the Plaza. Amused, Olivia followed behind it, watching with curiosity as it blended with the silhouettes of the night.

Although the shadow could clearly move at any speed it wanted, it now traveled just slowly enough for Olivia to follow its pace. It crossed Avilles de Menendez and paused at the river. Olivia crossed behind it, approaching the water.

When she heard the splashing of water hitting the wall she paused, thinking it might be a manatee or even a dolphin. Excited, she looked over the edge.

It was neither.

In the water a bare-chested, damp-haired Brad looked up at her with a wet smile.

"Are you shitting me?" she blurted out.

He gave her a warm grin.

"Do you stalk people often?" he asked with a bright smile.

"No. You're a first . . . Actually, I followed *him* here," she said as she pointed to the shadow.

Olivia took note of the pile of denim and leather on the shore and gave Brad a sideways glance.

"Oh, my God. Are you skinny dipping?" Just the thought of him naked in that water was enough to excite her.

"Yeah, so?"

"I guess I wouldn't have pegged you as the skinny dipping type. You seem a little too much of a . . . uh . . . tough guy for nude swimming."

The sound of laughter echoed off the water.

Brad looked to Olivia. His face went pale. Olivia started to giggle.

"What?" Brad asked confused.

"That look! You looked terrified, like the shadow is going to eat you alive or something."

"Well, yeah. That thing is making me crazy."

"Me, too, but it's not so bad. Feeling alive is a good thing . . ." she said as she started taking off her shirt.

"What are you doing?" Brad asked.

"You can't be having all the fun alone. I'm coming in, biker man," she said, revealing a black lace bra.

In general, being naked in the center of city, where she could be spotted by passersby or, worse, get arrested, was not an Olivia sort of thing to do, but the new Olivia was quite excited about the opportunity.

With a casual gesture, she reached behind and unhooked her bra clasp and tossed it into the grass.

"It feels so incredible out here, like the air can communicate directly with my skin."

In just her skirt, she reached her arms out and spun as if she were grabbing for the very molecules that made up the night air.

"You know, opening that box is the best thing that ever happened to me."

She began to pull off the skirt when she realized underneath it she wasn't wearing anything at all.

"What the fuck?" she laughed, looking around on the ground. "How does a girl lose her panties?" she asked.

"I can think of some ways." Brad smiled.

"No . . . I mean, I know I've been a little loopy lately, but how does one just lose her underwear?"

"Where'd you see them last?"

"I don't know . . ." she said, thoughtful.

"Screw it," she said. "Who cares." She peeked into the water and began to pull down her skirt.

Brad looked around, concerned. "I was actually thinking of getting out. It's getting late," Brad said, swimming to the concrete edge.

"Oh, no you don't," she said.

"What? I've been here a long time. It's time to head home." He rested his arms on the sides.

She kept smiling. "Not only do you *not* seem like the type of man to swim nude in the center of the city, you also don't seem like the type of man to pass up an opportunity. I mean, here I am this cute young woman with her breasts exposed in the open air, no panties to be seen, and you're this badass biker dude . . . wait, let me rephrase that . . . you're this *naked* badass biker dude." She eyed him and started to laugh. "Christ, we're like a cheesy romance novel waiting to be written." She spoke with playful conviction. "You know, Brad, I think you and I are meant to swim naked in this water together tonight. We are fated for it. And all you can say is 'It's getting late'?"

Brad didn't answer. He was done. The threat of falling to pieces again was too much for him to bear. He placed his hands on the edge and pulled himself onto the grass. He reached for his boxers. Olivia said nothing but watched with a smirk as he dressed.

He slipped on his t-shirt while watching her soft, playful eyes as they tracked him.

"Brad, did anyone ever tell you that you're magnificent?" she said." I mean, I know you're no spring chicken."

"Gosh, thanks," he said.

"No. No. It's not bad. You've got an incredible, irresistible male energy that . . ." she paused, looking for the word, ". . . that I just want to consume."

Olivia noted the scattering silver hairs that ran against his jawline, each one brightened in the moonlight, and she felt that relentless pang of hunger surge.

"Every one of your beard hairs is like an amazing piece of art work. Your face, your shoulders, your hands. What a sexual wonder you are."

Like a fox familiarizing itself with a new territory, she moved forward, cautious.

"You're bat-shit crazy," he said, shaking his head.

Brad had never been unsure of what he wanted from a woman, yet here he was with this water-nymph-like creature, both child and radiant woman at the same time. He had never met a woman who was free of pretenses, no falseness, just true to who she is in the open air.

As much as he wanted a part of what was in front of him, he was also very aware of the shadow's presence, its desire to unlock the things that needed to stay hidden. He refused to be dragged further into chaos.

"I just can't go there, Olivia," he said.

Olivia piped up, angered by his resistance, "How are you not affected by our shadow?" she asked. "Doesn't it make you in the least bit aroused?"

Brad spoke quietly, through his teeth. "It's not a question of attraction. I don't think the shadow does the same thing to me as it does to you."

There was a silent pause between them.

"Sure, it's affecting us differently, but that's because you're afraid. I'm not. Come on. Aren't you a little bit curious? We could have a really good romp, us two," Olivia pushed.

"I don't trust it. *It's* waiting to fuck me up."

"Brad, I've spent the last twenty-seven years of life terrified of everything, and now, finally, I feel free," Olivia said, her tone changing. "Because of this thing—whatever the hell it is—I'm alive."

Her eyes focused on his and she added softly, "You don't need to be afraid."

Olivia stepped towards him and brought herself in close. With soft curiosity, she brought her hand to Brad's arm and reached to his tattoo. He watched her closely but didn't resist. Then, with her index finger she slowly traced the image of the phoenix, winding her fingers along the lines of its body, delineating each of its fiery feathers as if her motions possessed the magic to make it come alive.

He watched as her delicate fingers rode up the line along his shoulder, to his neck, then his jaw. Then, with deliberate movement she brought her hand to his face and gently traced his chin, resting her fingers on the soft bristle of his beard.

"Fear is the only thing holding any of us back," she said.

Aware of her touch with fiery alertness, he tensed.

Almost on cue, the bellowing laugh made its way towards them, drawing their awareness to the hulking shadow as it moved closer.

Brad felt the heaviness return, a pain like a knife stabbing him from within. His body buckled as the agony of the past seemed to grow around him and he curled into himself in an aching sense of loss.

He looked to Olivia. Drowning in desperation, he wanted to reach out to the airy creature and cling to her. Instead he swallowed the pain.

"I have to go," he muttered.

Before she could pull him in, he finished getting dressed then stepped away into the dimness of the city, leaving Olivia and the shadow alone by the rippling waves.

Chapter 23

Back in her apartment, Olivia felt like she was treading in a pool of volatile feelings, darting between elation, shame, and desire. She felt as if she were doing everything wrong, but at the same time doing everything right. As she walked through the kitchen, she grabbed the box from the table and brought it with her into her bedroom.

The shadow had followed her home and now sat on her bed comfortably, its large body taking up residence in her small space. As she looked in her dresser mirror, its dark image was reflected behind her, observing her in silence.

She ran her palms against the texture of the box, rotating it within her hands, and wished to herself that she could somehow understand what was happening to her.

Her phone chimed three times, breaking her trance.

It was a chain of texts from Andrew.

"Can we talk?"

"Won't you reconsider?"

"I love you."

Feeling the creep of insanity return, she threw the phone onto the bed, and rather than crying her body surged into a fit of uncontrollable laughter, as if her life had become a wonderful joke. She lay back on her bed, and as she laughed, perhaps harder than she ever had before, her hysterics dissolved into tears.

She cried, not so much for the man she had lost, but for how strange and distant her life was becoming. And even though she was emerging bolder and brasher, she was also feeling more alone.

Chapter 24

By Monday morning, it appeared that the old Olivia had returned. She rose diligently at five forty-five, ate her routine breakfast, showered, and dressed in an unremarkable t-shirt and a pair of cargo shorts.

Before leaving the house she paused and looked at the box sitting on her night stand, wondering if the nearby Lightner Museum might have some answers about it. She tossed the box in her bag, headed outside, and walked to the bakery.

When she arrived at Eat it Too, the front door was unlocked. Loud music played from the back room and all the lights were on.

"Mandie?" she called out.

No one answered.

Olivia stepped to the kitchen. A stack of dishes sat at the sink, cake batter dried on the edges of the bowls. A coating of flour, dotted with drops of batter and a smear of hand prints, covered the main workspace.

Olivia turned down the volume on the speaker and, in a fury, grabbed the phone and dialed Mandie.

A message picked up after the second ring.

"Hey, it's me. Do what you have to do . . ."

Olivia tried to speak, but she couldn't. As angry as she was, she feared confrontation. She hung up.

A Jimi Hendrix tune played in the background.

There must be some kind of way out of here,

Said the joker to the thief,

There's too much confusion . . .

Friday night, when she had danced alone, the music had felt like a living, breathing creature, but now, as the dead musician sang on, it was gone. She felt dead, the song just a string of notes patched together to fill the holes in an empty existence. The hunger was gone. She needed the shadow back.

"Where are you?" she shouted to the room in hopes of summoning it. "You can't leave me." Nothing responded. The return to ordinariness was almost too much to bear.

She ran to her bag and pulled out the box. Grasping it tightly in her hands, she opened it then closed it several times.

"Come on," she said to the box, but again there was no reply.

As if she might be able to wipe away her hopelessness, she grabbed a rag and began washing down the counter. As she wiped with fervor, she noticed an odd imprint in the flour. There was something very distinct about the print, with its two touching ovals. In fact, to Olivia it looked remarkably like someone's ass. She looked at it again, and sure enough it had the smooth indentations of somebody's two round cheeks.

Pretending it wasn't what she thought, she brushed the flour into the dust pan then tossed the contents into the garbage can, watching as the powder fell inside the bag. Glancing in the trash, she did a double take. Amidst the food wrappers and discarded egg shells was a bottle of Wild Turkey and a spent condom.

"Oh, my God. Really?" she said out loud, her anger steaming as she tied up the trash tight and carried it at arm's length out the door.

This was a new low for Mandie.

Olivia swept then mopped the floors and bleached the counter tops two times over as she cringed at the thought of Tank riding her best friend atop the kitchen counter. She shuddered.

With nothing yet in the ovens, Olivia began assembling ingredients and measuring them into a mixing bowl. Mandie wouldn't arrive for hours, leaving Olivia all morning to prepare her confrontation. She wasn't going to cave this time. Mandie had to know how mad she really was.

She rehearsed it in her mind: *This was the last straw*, she would say to Mandie. *You have crossed the line. I have had enough.* Her lecture was to go on in detail about the importance of responsibility and loyalty and, of course, hygiene.

Around nine, the front door jingled and Mandie walked in wearing a navy, star-spangled halter dress, her poufy skirt accentuating her curved hips.

"Hey, girl! Morning," she said as she put down her purse on the counter right where the ass print had been.

"Tank and I had a blast getting stoned with you last night. He suggested we do it again soon."

Olivia just watched her friend as she spoke, amazed that she wouldn't even mention the disaster she and her boyfriend had left in their wake. But in the absence of the shadow, Olivia was unable to muster up the words. Rather than yelling, Olivia collapsed into tears.

"Oh, honey. What's wrong?" Mandie asked, walking over and putting her arm around Olivia.

Olivia looked up at her through blurred eyes. The rage was gone. Inferiority and weakness were in its place. Here was this elegant woman, her friend, who in spite of her wild negligence was infallible. People loved her, they responded to her, while Olivia was paralyzed by her emotions, one minute alive, one minute hopeless and grey. She had no idea who she was anymore.

She had no control over the words that came out of her mouth. "I'm sorry, Mandie."

"What for, hon?"

"For not being a good friend, for getting mad sometimes. I know you screw up, but you mean well, right?"

Mandie laughed. "You kidding? I'm a royal fuck up, and you're the only one who will tolerate it. You put up with all my shit. You're my bestie."

Olivia looked at her friend with a teary smile. She felt without spark, without fight. All she could do was yet again fake forgiveness.

Olivia went about her daily tasks, working in parallel with her friend. Noon arrived, time for Olivia's break, but she didn't care. With no appetite, she had no interest in going to Adella's shop.

She left Eat It Too, saying little to Mandie, and sat on a bench outside on the street. She took the wooden box from her bag and opened and closed it again, wishing as if this might beckon the dark soul to return.

Chapter 25

    Monday in the late morning, Brad sat alone in his shop. It was several hours before the Phoenix was to open. He let the silence of the store wrap around him like a protective cocoon, hiding him from the truth of his deteriorating life. Long shadows from a corner lamp played tricks on Brad's mind. He knew the creature was amongst those shadows, masked by the silhouettes of the room.

    Sitting on one of the shop stools, he curled his whole body over his phone. The blue light of the screen illuminated the tired lines of his face.

He scrolled through his list of contacts and stopped at "Rosalee." There was no last name, just a cell number. He selected it and typed a message.

"Hey. I'm sorry for not calling you back a few months ago."

He hit send then continued with his message.

"I was an ass. Please forgive me."

He then returned to his long list of names and stopped at "Sandra King." He remembered she was a tall brunette with legs to her neck. Five months back, they had met at the Iron Horse Saloon. Drunk to the gills, the two had had sloppy, drunken sex in the back of her car. It was all fun until she threw up on Brad.

After that night she had called him several times to apologize. He had never replied until now.

Just thinking of you.

He returned to the list and selected the name "Stephanie Severn."

When lunchtime arrived and Brad hadn't had any customers, yet, he figured it was just as well. He really wasn't in any mood to work. A light knock on the front door interrupted his thoughts, and Brad looked up to see Olivia standing at the door.

She looked drained, her lips curled into a frown. Realizing he still had his phone in his hand, he placed it at his side and walked over to let her in.

"I'm sorry to bother you."

He gave her an unreadable look as he tried to hide his misery.

"S'ok," Brad said, his mouth drawn in a stiff, straight line across his face. "So, what's up?"

"I . . . I . . . guess I was just wondering if you had seen the shadow lately."

Brad's phone beeped twice. He ignored it.

"Uh, I suppose . . . I dunno. I don't really keep tabs on it."

"But if it's not with me and it's not with you, where is it? Could it be gone?" Olivia asked, trying to suppress her worry.

She raised her eyes and noticed the shadow emerging from a side wall. Brad saw it, too, and gritted his jaw. His phone blipped several times as three more texts came in. He picked up the phone and glanced at one from a girl named Shel that read:

"You're forgiven . . . you wanna do dinner!?"

Brad felt like he was teetering, unable to move, as if movement in any direction would shatter what little semblance of order he had left. What the hell was he doing?

Brad looked at Olivia.

"I'm so tired. All of this, it's overwhelming," Olivia said, wanting to fall on to him, rest her head on his shoulder, but she kept her distance.

"I know things feel worse, but they aren't," Brad stated firmly, trying to convince himself as much as her. "You're just tired, overwhelmed. Everything that's happened . . . it is a lot to deal with. But it will be okay."

Olivia saw through his ruse. Brad was a man on the run. She knew. The shadow's chaos made him vulnerable while it made her strong.

He walked away from her and returned to his stool. He picked up the phone and began scrolling through his list again.

"Who are you texting?" she asked.

"You don't want to know."

"Maybe I do."

He looked at her coldly.

"It's all the girls I've ever fucked."

Olivia frowned.

Brad continued. "All I can think is that the shadow is here to punish me . . . maybe for all the women I've screwed and ignored. I'm thinking maybe if I can get their forgiveness, I can clear myself of this curse."

Olivia looked at him, her brow furrowed. "You think the shadow gives a damn about the women you slept with?"

The shadow let out a slow, warm chuckle from the back of the room and Olivia felt its turmoil seep into her like a drug injected into her vein.

She tilted her head back and began to laugh.

"Finally!" she grinned as she reached her arms up like antennas collecting the radiance of the room. She then brought them in and hugged herself. "You have no idea how good this feels."

She looked to Brad, his lips formed into a slight frown, and felt the urge to move closer, to twist her fingers through the locks of his hair, then wrap herself around him and take in his scent.

"You know what this shadow makes me want most?" she asked.

Brad grasped his phone tighter.

She continued, "More than chocolate fudge . . . more than dancing in the moonlight . . . more than life itself?"

Brad stood rigid. He didn't speak.

He knew the answer, but she said it anyway.

"I want you!"

Brad's expression remained stiff.

"Why can't you feel it?" Olivia begged. "That passion! Won't you give in to it? Please?" She reached out her hand to his ear and toyed with his earring.

"So, what say you, biker man?" she asked.

Brad could feel Olivia's heat as she stood just inches from him.

Brad pulled back. "I'm sorry, Olivia. I can't."

"So that's it? Just 'No'?" Olivia looked dejected.

"This thing is waiting for me to slip up. It feeds on my vulnerability. You know as well as I do, this shit doesn't make any sense. Having sex with you . . . even being around you is compromising my stability."

"That's just stupid."

"I don't want to be open. There's too much shit in there. It will eat me alive. I know."

"Being open isn't bad."

"Are you sure about that? I mean, look at you all over the place. Kissing that dirt bag, *Buzz?* Seriously?" He looked at her with a hard stare. "But, I get it. You're already vulnerable. I bet you've always been that way. You don't fear it because you have less far to fall than I do."

"So you're saying I'm weak?"

"I didn't say you're weak. I mean you're fragile . . . delicate . . ."

Olivia wrinkled her brow.

"Is that what you think of me? Just a vulnerable, out-of-control woman? That's how I come off to you?"

"No . . . that's . . ." Brad began, but before he could say anymore Olivia was out the door, heading back up the street.

"Fuck!" he yelled, and he side swiped a tray of inks across the floor, spreading reds, blues, and blacks across the tile.

The shadow leaned back on the couch and chuckled deeply.

"And fuck you!" Brad yelled, pointing at the dark creature. The shadow rose. Now several feet taller than he was, it loomed beside him.

Brad heard two people talking out front and cringed when he realized he was hearing the sound of Buzz's weasely voice. He and Courtney were at the door.

"Hi, Brad," Courtney said as she stepped in.

Brad barely looked up at her.

Buzz scanned Brad up and down. "Hey, man, you look like shit. You partying too hard or something?" he asked as he glanced down at the inks spread across the floor. Brad gave him a glare.

"What's up your ass?" Buzz asked and walked out of the main room to the stock room, leaving Courtney alone with Brad for a moment.

"Hey," she said, "I want to thank you for not firing Buzz yesterday."

"Didn't I?"

"No. He said you just sent him home."

Brad frowned.

"Yeah, I suppose . . . well, you're welcome," Brad said.

"You're great," Courtney leaned forward and kissed him on the cheek.

"Yeah. I'm great." Brad said, rubbing his eyes with the heels of his hands.

"I saw Gramps this morning. He seems okay. He's still pale and doesn't have any energy. The nurses are still feeding him applesauce and shit."

"Oh, yeah?" Brad asked.

"Yeah, but I don't think it's because he can't handle a spoon, I think it's because he likes having the nurses feed him."

"Dirty mother fucker," Brad muttered to himself with an amused smile. He bent down to clean the spilled ink.

"You gonna go see him today? He's been asking about you."

"Yeah. Yeah. I will. Just been really busy." The thought of returning to that hospital made his stomach turn.

"It'll make his day." Courtney smiled and poked her head into the back room. "Hey, Buzz, I'm starving. I'm going to order a pizza."

"Pizza sounds good. I'll go in on that with you. No mushrooms," Buzz said from the other side of the wall.

"No problem, hot stuff," Courtney responded.

Courtney placed an order while Buzz came out of the back room, carrying a box of rubber gloves. Brad had no intention of letting him work, but in his current state he was unable to muster the words to tell the idiot to go home.

"The pizza guy said he'll deliver it in half an hour," Courtney said.

She then took a lock of her boyfriend's scraggly blond hair in her hand and said, "I'm you're girl, right Buzz?"

"Yeah. Of course," he said.

She leaned over and kissed him. "You're acting funny lately, Buzz. I hope everything is okay. You know you're, like, my everything, sweetie."

He shrugged her off.

Brad rose, jolted with anger, as the shadow's demon laughter returned. Holding back his now rampant rage at Courtney's and Buzz's blatant hypocrisy, he stormed to the back.

In the storage room, Brad sifted through the new texts on his phone, reading all the women's replies. A new one from Janice said,

"I remember you! My apartment on New Year's!"

About thirty minutes passed, and a loud crash came from the other room followed by yelling. Courtney barged into the stock room with tears in her eyes, her melted makeup giving her the appearance of a sad raccoon. Brad's shadow was behind her.

"Brad, the pizza guy is here and Buzz won't pay his share for the pizza. I've got no cash on me. I'm totally broke and I know he's got, like, fifty in his wallet."

"Court, this is not my problem," Brad said, the voices in his head laughing louder than before.

Buzz shouted from the other room, "Get your ass out here, Courtney!"

"Brad, just help me . . ." Courtney said, pleading with him.

Brad rose slowly and stepped into the studio. The pizza delivery man stood by the door with a nervous look on his face, a pizza box in hand.

Buzz said, "I'm not paying for your fucking pizza, Courtney. I said no mushrooms and you ordered them anyway. The whole fucking thing is covered in them."

Courtney turned to Brad, "Can you just pay this time?" she asked.

Wanting it all to be over, Brad reluctantly reached for his wallet. As he did, Buzz yelled, "No! Brad, this is Courtney's problem. She ordered the God damned pizza. She's got to pay. I know she's got spare cash, I saw it there this morning."

"What were you doing in my wallet, Buzz?" Courtney screamed.

"Just keeping tabs on you, bitch."

"Oh, yeah, well you haven't been keeping a very good watch. You don't know shit about *me and Brad*."

Brad felt his stomach drop.

"What do you mean *'you and Brad'*?" Buzz asked, a little waver in his voice.

The pizza guy stood close to the door, apparently not sure if he should forget the money and run or stick around to see what would happen.

Courtney stepped towards Brad and said with pride, "Brad and I slept together."

Buzz stepped towards Courtney, pulled his arm back, and punched her in the face, knocking her to the floor.

From the ground she hissed, "You'll never be as good a fuck as he is."

"Shut up, bitch." Buzz turned to Brad, fuming, "Is this true?"

Brad looked from Buzz to Courtney and, in place of weakness, he felt a burgeoning power, as if his role of being a decent man dissolved away.

Brad growled with a sinister smile, "You know what, you ass wipe?" he said, feeling the passion of a wildfire within him, "Courtney is absolutely right . . . you will never be as good a fuck as me." He laughed with power. ". . . and, yeah, I did your girl. I took her ripe little ass from behind right on that chair." He pointed to the chair Buzz was leaning on.

Buzz charged Brad with ferocity. He brought his scrawny arm back, curled his hand into a fist, and lunged forward with a punch.

Brad deflected the ineffectual swing then wrapped his arm around Buzz's neck and held him tightly in a choke hold until he was gasping for breath. Brad laughed like a man with nothing to lose. It had been so long since he had savored the feeling of raw anger, and in that moment it tasted good.

"You know what, you asshole? I'm done being the good guy. I made a promise to Courtney that I wouldn't fire you, but fuck promises. You are a putrid ghost of a man, without the wits to tie your own fucking shoes. And, let me tell you, if you even think about touching Olivia again, I will kill you."

He released Buzz and watched him as he fell, straining for air, a look of panic on his face."

"I . . . I didn't even know she was your girl."

Brad, done with Buzz, turned to the pizza guy, "I'll take that pizza now."

The delivery boy's mouth was wide open. He said nothing, just handed over the box and sped out the door. Courtney stood, like a wilted flower, glancing back and forth between the two men.

Brad returned to the store room, shutting the door behind him. Alone, he closed his eyes and whispered to himself.

"I've had enough. I am done with you." The shadow's laugh began again, only this time it was so loud he had to cover his ears.

Brad stood and walked to the front room where he found Courtney tending to Buzz's wounds while crying to him, "I'm sorry, I'm sorry."

Brad, disgusted, turned to the two of them and said, "I'm done," and walked out the door.

Chapter 26

Brad had no plan, no idea where he was going to land next.

As he wandered down the street, he paused at Eat It Too and looked in the window. He saw two women moving about. He grabbed the door handle and walked in. The air conditioning, running high, seemed to cool more than just his body; it calmed his blazing mind as well.

Inside, the bakery was decorated like the interior of a treasure box. Bottle caps, plastic toys, mardi gras beads adorned the walls. Surrounding a large mirror was a set of old magnetic alphabet letters, just like the one he had had as kid. Spelled out in colorful letters were the words "Eat My Cake."

From the back came an Amazon of a woman with breasts fit for display in a museum. He found it difficult to keep his eyes off them.

"Hi! Welcome to Eat it Too," she said, sizing him up.

Brad freed his eyes and glanced at the case to see rows of cupcakes, topped with marzipan limbs, candied skulls, and plastic insects. He recognized the zombie mermaid tattoo on the woman's arm that his former employee, Donny, had done about a year back. She seemed to fit so perfectly in this place, as if she could have been another artifact on the wall.

"Can I help you with something?" she asked, appearing to recognize him, too.

"Yeah," he said, looking around past a beaded curtain. "I'm looking for a girl named Olivia."

"*Really?*" the woman asked, curiosity beaming out of her.

"Yeah. Is she here?"

"Why, yes, she is," the woman said. She gave him a knowing eye as she slipped behind a curtain.

"Olivia, there's a *man* here to see you," Brad heard her say.

"Really?" a familiar voice asked. "Who?"

"I dunno. Some guy who's inked to the nines."

The two women's voices became hushed.

"So you weren't kidding. The *new* Olivia is into bikers? And pretty decent looking ones at that."

Olivia peeked her head out. It was apparent to Brad as he looked at her that her life with the shadow was taking its toll. She looked at him with a flat glare.

"Hi," she said.

"Hey."

"Why are you here?" she asked, as she noticed the shadow slipping into the store.

They looked at each other.

"Apparently, Mr. Reaper followed me here." He said with a frown.

"It's not a reaper," Olivia spoke in hushed words. "It's a muse . . ."

The shadow chuckled, and Olivia felt the hollowness in her belly fill with power.

The two paused as Mandie emerged and pretended to busy herself with cupcakes in the case.

"Why are you here?" Olivia asked again, straight faced.

"I don't know. I just sorta ended up here. I'm sorry about what I said. I take it back, you're not a wimp. This thing's got me so fucked up . . . I just . . ."

"So, how do you two know each other?" Mandie broke into the conversation.

Brad and Olivia glanced at each other.

What could she possibly say to Mandie? Her life was too ridiculous to explain.

Olivia looked to Brad, and he lightened up. The two smiled together as if sharing an inside joke.

"What?" Mandie asked, wanting to be in on it.

Brad, with a surprising amount of believability, explained, "She came in to see about getting a tattoo at my shop."

Olivia looked at him, surprised.

"Really? Of what?" Mandie still wanted in on the joke.

"Do tell," Olivia smiled.

"A pirate . . . a one-legged one with an eye patch and a bow in his beard."

Olivia struggled to keep from laughing out loud.

"A pirate? *Olivia?* Really?" Mandie asked.

"Oh, yeah. Totally." Olivia played along. "Mandie, don't you remember me saying how much I love pirates? Especially the one-legged ones. Mmm . . . hot."

"Not really," Mandie said, feeling dejected as she realized her friend and this new man were playing her for a fool. "I'm going to let you two talk about whatever you have to talk about, and I'll just go decorate some cupcakes."

As she stepped behind the curtain, Brad let out a loud "Argh!" like a cartoon pirate.

Olivia burst out laughing.

"I don't think she was too happy with our little joke," Olivia said.

"Joke? There's no joke. You're getting a pirate tattoo," Brad smiled.

Olivia whapped him on the arm.

Brad just shook his head with a grin and promptly changed the subject. "Ever hear of the Fairchild Oak?"

"Nope. Is it somewhere around here?" Olivia asked.

"Sort of . . . I'm taking you there."

"Now?"

"Yes. I need to get away. Maybe if we leave quick enough we can outrun that God damned shadow and you and I will both come to our senses."

"But, I need to be at the shop."

"You don't have any customers. It's too hot to buy fucking zombie cupcakes or whatever you make. Besides, your friend can keep things going. Hell, her tits alone could keep the shop running."

"You noticed those, huh?"

"How could I not? So, leave miss booby-lady and come on."

"I don't know. I don't do this kind of thing."

"Where's that crazy girl in leather I was talking to the other day? She'd do it. Come on." He gently touched her bare shoulder, and the warmth from his hand seemed to melt into her skin, giving her an odd sense of calm.

"Okay, let's do this," she said, and she peeked behind the curtain into the kitchen.

"I'm taking the afternoon off," she called.

"What? What about the Milbournes' order?" Mandie called back.

"You can do it. It's only three dozen. I do orders that size all the time when Pogo's got digestive issues." Before Mandie could defend herself, Olivia returned to the front room.

"See ya," she called back.

She grabbed her bag and turned to Brad.

"Ready?" she asked, giving him a starry smile.

"Most definitely. Let's go get my bike," he said.

"Your motorcycle?" Olivia asked for clarification.

"You think I ride a bicycle?" he laughed. "Come on,"

Brad walked with Olivia along a red-bricked path down the narrow side streets. They made their way past the Cathedral Basilica, then past the college, behind the red-roofed Lightner Museum. Parked beside a tree was Brad's black Harley, his golden phoenix emblem painted brightly on the tank.

"It's beautiful!" she said. "I didn't even notice this painting the other night." She touched it with reverence as if it was a gem on display in a museum. "You know, I've read up on totem animals of the Native Americans. The phoenix must be your totem, guiding you through the mysteries of life."

Brad smiled. "It's just a bird. The shadow's got you fucked up."

"It's not just a bird, it's a symbol of self-discovery, renewal," she said with a toying grin.-"You know what this whole phoenix thing means, don't you?"

"No, what?"

"It means you're being looked out for. Whenever you hit rock bottom, you're born again. You've got nothing to fear."

Brad shook his head in amusement then changed the subject. "Have you ever ridden on a bike before?"

"Does my neighbor's Vespa count?"

"No," Brad chuckled.

"Okay. Well, then, no. Come on, let's do this, biker man!" Olivia said, eagerly lifting her leg over the seat.

Brad's bike started up with the telltale Harley roar. Olivia had heard this rumble a thousand times before, but never from right on top of it. This was the call of rebels, outlaws, and people who sought out wild adventure. She associated it with the black-leathered visitors who arrived in droves twice a year, yet here she was, legs straddled over the rumbling machine, ready to go on a journey with a man whose rough and wild life was so foreign to her.

The bike's vibration filled her body with electric intensity, awakening her from the inside out. A broad smile grew across her face as Brad pulled out onto the highway.

The long road known as A1A stretched along the Florida coastline. Much of the coast was dotted by grand, four-story homes facing the ocean. Once in a while, they passed a billboard or two promoting beachside real estate or open-deck bars with an ocean view.

Olivia kept her hands firm on Brad's sides, secretly enjoying the warm feeling of cupping her hands on his hips. With the road congested by summer tourists, they had to stop and start repeatedly as folks looked for ideal beach parking. Once past the bustle, they reached the open road and Brad accelerated past the speed limit. Olivia felt her body tugged backward aggressively. Without thinking, she wrapped her arms around him, holding tight, her chest squeezed hard against his back. He looked back and gave her a smile.

When they approached the small town of Flagler Beach, their view widened with an expansive spread of the Atlantic on their left. Ocean breaks, dotted with surfers and playful beachgoers, set the mood for a lazy afternoon.

In her eight years in Florida, Olivia had never been on this stretch of highway. There was something simple, less hurried than the money-making bustle of Saint Augustine. She nestled her face into Brad's shoulder, taking in his warm, leathery scent.

Brad took the next bend with a playful swerve, turning off the main highway onto High Bridge Road. Their ocean view was now replaced with palms and gnarly subtropical oaks. The trees' arms stretched beyond the woods and over the road, creating a shaded archway above their heads.

Brad slowed the bike as they approached a gravel road. He pulled into a parking lot, found a spot, and killed the engine. Olivia looked around at the open park while inhaling the green scent. A mammoth tree robed in moss stood as the park's focal point.

With a trunk the circumference of eight men's arms linked hand to hand, its branches curved outward over the park and to the blue sky. Up above, nestled in the leafy boughs, ferns and wild orchids grew, living their symbiotic existence in the tree.

Over the centuries, several of the giant limbs had grown downward instead of up, finding their way back into the ground and returning as roots.

"Oh, wow," Olivia said, getting off the bike. She walked towards the tree.

"Pretty amazing, huh?" Brad said.

"How old is this thing?"

"Two thousand . . . some say more."

"Jesus." She rested her hand on its trunk. Brad stood beside her, admiring the branches that reached six stories high.

"Some say the Fairchild Oak is haunted. A guy in the early 1900s killed himself right near the tree. He was deep in debt. Offed himself with poison, just so his wife could get the life insurance money," Brad said.

"Damn," Olivia said, putting her face up against the trunk.

Olivia looked to Brad, who was keeping a cautious eye out, as if at any time the shadow would arrive to ruin their fun.

"I haven't seen the shadow. If that's what you're looking for," she said

"I know, but I feel it."

"Me, too. I feel it when I'm with you, even though it's not here." She touched the tree again. "You know, I swear I can feel the tree's energy, like its pulse is tapping into my veins. It's amazing," she said.

She reached out and placed Brad's hand against the trunk, hoping to distract him from his worries.

"Here. Feel."

Brad looked at her. Her blond locks were wild and unkempt from the ride, her eyes revealing the joy she felt at being alive in that moment. He smiled, feeling a sort of calm he hadn't felt in years. Then, as if detecting a person's quiet pulse, he felt it—the life blood of the oak began a delicate beat that built, stronger and stronger, pounding through his being.

"Damn!" Brad said.

"See! It's *all* frickin' alive, these woods, the birds, the plants. It's got voice, and because of that shadow we're open to it."

Brad brought his other hand to the tree and rested for a moment.

"You know how insane this is, right?" Brad said, interrupting the silence.

"I know. I've always been sort of a rationalist, but now I don't know. I just feel so alive. You feel it, too. I know you do. The shadow is bringing us closer to who we are."

Brad smiled at her. Being in the presence of Olivia's bright optimism, whether shadow-induced or not, made things feel not so bad. He removed his hand from the tree and reached out to her, intertwining his fingers into hers.

"You're like some sort of a woodland creature . . . like a tree nymph," he said.

Olivia laughed.

"You look magical, too . . . like . . . I suppose . . . a unicorn!"

"A unicorn? Gee, thanks. Of all the mythical creatures you could have chosen to describe me, you picked that?"

"Oh. No, don't get me wrong . . . you're like the most manly of unicorns." Olivia laughed. "A handsome, extremely muscular one!"

"I guess I can settle for that," he said. He scanned the tree above him. "Hey, you wanna do something fun?"

"I'm game," Olivia grinned.

He walked to one of the limbs that touched the ground and pulled himself up on it.

Olivia was never good at climbing trees—or anything that challenged her physical abilities for that matter—but the sense of adventure was still boiling in her. With attentiveness, she pulled herself up and shimmied across the tree, trying not to look down.

Hand over hand, foot over foot she climbed until she was just one branch away from Brad, easily thirty feet in the air. She stopped and, with caution, settled her back against a thick branch, her feet balancing at an intersecting joint.

"Now, look," he said as he pointed towards the west.

Cautiously she took her eyes away from the trunk and followed his hand. Above the tree line she could see for miles in every direction. The sun was setting over the marshlands, dipping down behind the islands of mangroves. Pinks, oranges, and blues spread in rays across the sky. There was a silence between them as they watched the sky shift in hues.

She looked to Brad as he appeared deep in thought.

He eventually spoke: "I don't know if I can keep doing this, Liv."

"Doing what? Hanging out with me? Because, personally, I'm sort of enjoying this," she smiled.

"No. The shadow. I don't like who it's making me."

"I don't see it doing anything horrible to you right now," Olivia said. "It's leaving us alone. We're having a nice evening."

"Yeah, now. But, even with it not here, I can feel it wrapped in me, like its grubby hands are wrapped around inside me. It's bringing out shit in me that I'd prefer to keep buried."

"I know. It's bringing out stuff in me, too. I stole, like, $300 dollars' worth of clothes, and I can't remember a thing about it. I'm sure I'll be black-listed from The Cat's Meow, but for some reason I just don't care. I'm feeling more in tune, more alive than ever."

"Yeah, well, what if I don't want to feel more alive?" Brad asked with a frown.

"I don't think we have a choice. You can either be pulled to it kicking and screaming, or you can face it head on. Either way, it's coming."

He reached out and brushed his hand through her hair. "You know, Liv, for being such a flighty nymph, a lot of wise words come out of your mouth."

She looked out at the sky and smiled, amused by his teasing, and felt his warm body move in close.

With a hunger that didn't even feel like his own, he moved in and brought his lips to hers. Olivia's grip on the tree softened, and their lips locked, slow and passionate.

Olivia pulled back, a drunken look in her eyes. The pink light from the setting sun illuminated her face in a warm glow, causing her to look foreign and beautiful. Somehow in her beauty she also appeared dangerous, like she herself was the cause of the chaos around them.

They heard the sound of a car rolling on gravel and looked down to see an SUV pull up. Stabilizing herself, Olivia watched as four teenagers climbed out of the car, carrying a heavy cooler out with them.

"We're setting a bad example being up here," Olivia whispered.

"I don't think they're here to climb trees," he said, watching the kids pull cans of Budweiser from the case.

With the setting sun, the branches were now in shadow. Brad made his way down with caution, helping Olivia along the way. The couple leapt out of the tree, inadvertently giving the teenagers a scare.

"Don't climb the tree," Brad said as he winked at them and pointed to a large park sign that Olivia hadn't seen before.

"Yeah, thanks for the tip," one of the teens said.

The couple got on the bike and rode away.

Chapter 27

Brad rode the same route back home. However, rather than looking at the scenery this time, Olivia chose to nestle her face deep in the warmth of Brad's leather vest, letting the wind play games with her hair from behind.

As they returned to the old city, they crossed the Bridge of Lions and were greeted by the sparkling lights of the park.

Brad turned back to Olivia and shouted over the roar of the motor.

"Our little adventure isn't over, yet."

"What do you mean?" she called forward.

"You'll see."

Brad pulled down a side street and backed his bike into an empty spot. Olivia hopped off and waited for him.

"So? What's the plan?" she asked.

"I'm not sayin'. Just come with me."

As they walked down the back streets towards Saint George, they passed numerous bars, each with their own flavor of music spilling onto the street.

They arrived at the Phoenix, and Brad unlocked the door and flipped on the lights.

Having never hung out in a tattoo shop before, Olivia looked around, curious. She took her time to peruse a flash rack of sample tattoo images: flaming eyeballs, bloody daggers, demon skulls. Unimpressed, she wandered over to the couch and plunked herself down.

"Okay. You've got me. Why are we here?" she said.

Brad walked over, picked up his tattoo machine on the counter, sat down on a wheeled stool, and placed his foot on a floor pedal. An electric hum filled the room.

"We're here to get you that tattoo."

"What tattoo?"

"The pirate one!" He said, rolling himself over to his collection of inks.

"Oh, no. That was a joke." She put her hands up defensively.

"But, what's your friend going to say when you come to work on Monday without Captain Morgan on your ass?"

"Oh lord! Don't even think about it."

A dark chuckling came from the back of the room.

"Fuck, no!" she said in response to the shadow.

"Oh, come on," Brad said, tapping the pedal a few more times, enjoying the terrified face she made as it buzzed.

"Look, I respect your profession, but I'm not comfortable with this. Brad, I need you to promise, if this shadow-thing takes me away into la la land and I start begging for a God damned tattoo of Black Beard, you won't do it."

Brad looked at the shadow and put down the gun. "Promise," he said.

"But . . ." A crimson smile slid across her face. "If I was to ever get one, I do have an idea."

"Oh, yeah?" Brad asked intrigued.

"Since the whole box thing started, I sort of feel like I've been cracked open. Even without the shadow around I'm feeling more adventurous, less afraid."

"Yeah? So? What are you thinking, fearless Olivia?" he asked, glancing over to the shadow.

"An osprey. I see them on my beach walks all the time," Olivia said. "And I saw one out by the river the night of the crash."

"That's funny. I saw one the other day in the graveyard. I think I have its feather here." He pulled the fine white feather from the pocket of his jeans.

Olivia's eyes went wide.

"This is really an osprey feather?"

"Yeah, I watched it fall off of the bird and picked it up from the ground. Weird shit." Brad wheeled himself over to the shop's laptop.

He looked up "osprey," and a slew of photos came up showing the large hawks perched in trees, flying over the ocean, diving for fish.

"I love how they can be graceful and delicate, yet also so incredibly strong," Olivia said with a wistful tone.

"Hmm . . . like you."

Olivia smiled. "I'm relieved to know I'm no longer a vulnerable wimp in your mind."

"Yeah. I can see the other side of you . . . you don't scare easily. Hell, if you had to duke it out with that shadow I'm pretty sure you'd win."

"Probably," Olivia laughed. "Hey, what about this one?" she interrupted herself.

The image of an osprey filled the screen, its wings spread out, the tips fanning into articulated feathers. As if brushed with paint, a black "mask" gave its eyes a look of intensity and determination.

"I like it, but what if we make it more stylized, more you," Brad said, pulling out a pen and a piece of paper. From a few strokes emerged a bird on the page, even more graceful-looking than the one on the screen.

"We could incorporate some design in the center," Brad said. "Is there a style you're drawn to? Native American, Mehndi, Celtic?"

She thought for a moment, then she reached for her bag and pulled out the box.

Brad found himself tensing when he saw it. He hadn't seen it since that night at the bridge.

Olivia picked up on this and smiled. "Don't worry. Whatever was going to come out already did."

Olivia pointed to the intricately carved vine pattern. "How about this? I love all these curves and curls. My guess is it's Spanish, maybe 16th century."

Brad looked at her, amused.

"Spanish, 16th century— really? And how do you come to this conclusion, Professor Liv?"

"I was an art history major. I was supposed to open an art gallery someday but sort of got side tracked . . ."

"Aren't weird cupcakes art enough for you?" Brad smiled.

"Yeah. Right." Olivia frowned. "So? Can you do the design?"

"Yeah. For sure. Do you really want it? No shadow speaking, just you?"

Olivia thought for a moment. "Yeah. Just me."

Brad worked for about twenty minutes, his pencil taking charge of his hand as he sketched. Olivia waited, trying to calm her nerves by flipping through the pages of a magazine featuring scantily clad, tattoo-covered women on motorcycles.

"Okay, I think it's done," he said, and he walked it over to her. She held the paper in her hands and inspected it.

The osprey's wings were outstretched into two elegant arcs, its feathers fanning outward like fingers reaching to the ends of the earth. The core of its body was articulated with vine-like swirls that mimicked the ones carved into the box. The image told a story of freedom and grace.

"So?" he asked.

"I love it," she said.

Brad gave her a satisfied smile. He had worked hard to make the drawing reflect her essence. It was her to the utmost.

She gave him a look of confidence. "Let's do this!"

Brad went to his copier and printed out a stencil. Olivia stepped over to his booth, sat down beside him, and watched as he divvied the ink into small cups: white and black and a hint of pink, for the accents.

"Put your arm here," he said, patting a small, padded stand wrapped in cellophane. Following his direction, she rested her arm on the stand, turning the bare skin of her forearm upward. He wiped her arm clean with rubbing alcohol then carefully laid the stencil down.

He pulled up the paper, revealing a purple outline of his design.

"How's that?" he asked.

She nodded with a nervous smile.

"Good?" he asked, confirming her nod. "You only get one chance at this."

"No. It's good. I just can't believe I'm doing this."

"You're braver than you think you are."

Olivia watched with anticipation as Brad assembled the machine and positioned a bright light so that it illuminated her bare skin. He dipped the machine in the ink and brought the needle to her wrist. He placed his foot on the pedal. A low-frequency hum filled the room as the needle pulsed in a blur of motion.

Olivia felt her heartbeats intensify.

Brad paused. "Ready?" he asked.

"Okay," she said with a tremble in her voice. Panicked, internal voices warned her against what she was about to do.

In her head, the old Olivia begged, *You will regret this for the rest of your life. Stop this now, before it's too late,* but the Olivia in the moment silenced her. This is who she was becoming. It was too late to go back. She had stepped out on that ledge and leapt days before. Her descent into a new life had already begun.

Brad dipped the needle into the black vial, but just as he lowered the needle down to Olivia's forearm, a booming laughter filled the room. It felt one hundred times louder than the irritating voices in her head. This one had command and power.

Olivia felt it first: a rise within her body, like a livid heat, her blood churning, her palms hot and achy. She looked at Brad in a moment of desperation.

"You don't have to give in to it, Olivia. Fight it. Be strong," he said

But, as he spoke, he felt it, too; a hollow ache, empty powerlessness. Brad gritted his teeth.

"It's got you, too," she said as her eyes brightened and she felt the fiery impulse of the beast.

Before Brad could make his first line, Olivia jerked back and looked around, agitated, like a drug addict looking for her fix.

"You know what? I don't think I'm supposed to be here, to be doing this, not now. The shadow has bigger plans for me. It wants me out of this place. It wants me free." She rose and headed to the door.

"What are you doing?" Brad asked.

"I need to get out of here. This place is too stuffy. I'm itching for something more," she said as if her own skin confined her. "I need to go."

Brad just looked at her.

"Come on, biker man. It's time to live."

With the machine still vibrating in his hand, Brad stared, paralyzed by a kaleidoscope of emotions. He wanted to control this woman in front of him, slow her down. She needed to sit, to stay, but here in the shop she was like an imprisoned tiger thrashing wildly, trying to find its way out.

"You coming?" she asked, her hand on the door handle, but he was unable to speak, he was being swallowed alive. He needed her back. She was the ballast in this sea of chaos, but before he could act, the darkness of his mind consumed him and he fell, drowned in his own painful dreams.

Olivia didn't even look back as she headed out onto the street.

CHAPTER 28

Saint Augustine, Florida

December 31st, 1923

Cora looked up to the sky, appreciating the spray from the fountain that reached as high as the palms. A fine, wet mist falling from above landed on her face. What a novelty it was to have a fountain running in late December. When she left New York two days ago on the Florida East Coast Railroad, it was eleven degrees.

Like a child, she dipped her fingers into the pool and swished her hand around, turning the water into a fury of turquoise and blues.

Women in brightly colored matching hats and dresses strode by, enjoying the Florida air.

OPEN SOULS

Cora shifted her skirt and pulled out of her pocket a gold watch that hung from her neck. Six o'clock in the evening. Madeline's train was due to arrive at any time. Cora hadn't seen her best friend and former boarding school roommate in two whole years, and she was eager to catch up. College had changed her, and she wondered if Paris had done the same for Madeline.

Beside Cora, the nearby bushes blossomed with raspberry-colored hibiscus. Having only seen the exotic flower in paintings to this point, she approached the bushes to get a closer look at the blooms of the living specimen. As she did, a large grey and white bird swooped out of the sky like an angel with a plan. It dove for something beneath the bush, then rose up with nothing in its claws.

Wondering if it had struck a mouse, Cora looked under the hibiscus. There was no mouse, but tossed haphazardly, lying on its side beneath a bright pink flower, was a wooden box. She looked around to make sure no one was watching as she bent down and pulled it out.

The old wooden box was bound with metal re-enforcers and carved with ornate flowers and leaves. On the front it said something in Latin.

"No more chaos," she translated. For once in her life, her two years of studying Latin had come in handy.

Sensing this was more than just an ordinary box, she started to unhook the clasp.

"Boo!" a voice said from behind.

Cora jumped. She turned around to see Madeline standing with open arms, her cheeks rosy, her skin bright. Cora concealed the box by her side.

"Madeline!" *she said, giving Madeline a hug.*

"Well, if you aren't just a picture of beauty!" *Madeline said.*

"Oh, no. Me? Are you kidding?" *Cora said, though she always found a secret pleasure in her friend's praise.*

Madeline's dress was bright and flowy, cut right below her knee. Her hair was dramatically cropped into a short black bob. Madeline's new life in Paris was obviously influencing her fashion, as she now looked more like the Parisian women Cora met at her father's dinner parties than a New York girl.

A dark-skinned man wearing an orange jacket stood behind them, weighted down by three suitcases. Madeline ignored him.

"I can't believe we're doing this!" *she squealed.* "Your stodgy father actually came through!"

"I worked him well." *Cora smiled.*

Looking around, Madeline asked, "Tell me, have you seen any delicious men, yet?"

"Hmm. A few. Look there."

Two young men wearing knickers and flat caps strode by.

The tall one tipped his hat to the girls, and Madeline grinned devilishly.

"That's my husband-to-be! I've already decided," Madeline giggled. "Now come, shall we find our room?" She reached out to her friend and they walked arm in arm towards the grand hotel. Palm trees and other tropical plants filled the exquisite courtyard.

"Oh! It's Louis Comfort Tiffany," Madeline said pointing out the stained glass door adorned with an angel. "Daddy had all of our fixtures commissioned by him."

Cora gave her a half smile. Madeline's family was always a few steps above her own.

The girls entered a palatial foyer with white marble floors. Romanesque pillars climbed two stories high.

At the front desk they were greeted by a man in a maroon jacket and white gloves. The man carrying Madeline's bags put them down.

"I trust you know about our New Year's Eve Ball, tonight?" the manager said.

"We do!" Cora answered.

"Well, you chose the right place to welcome in the new year." He smiled. "We have some of the finest accommodations around. There will be dancing on the second and third floor mezzanine and swimming below. Our pool is the largest indoor pool in the world."

"Wonderful," Madeline said. "We're very much looking forward to going for a swim."

"Well, Happy New Year to you both. I do hope you enjoy your stay."

The girls were lead to their third-floor room, which was hung with red velvet drapes and had a bedspread to match. As soon as the bellhop left, the girls jumped onto their respective beds and laid beneath the gold brocade canopies.

"Oh, thank heavens. I'm sick of traveling," Madeline said, unlacing her shoes. "So are we going to see the town before dinner?"

"It's not much of a town," Cora said. "A bunch of old ruins. Drab. Drab. Drab." She laughed.

"Well, we're not here to see horrid prisons and alligator farms, anyway. We're here to catch up—oh, and to find rich men, of course," Madeline said.

"Yes. Men," Cora squealed. "So, please tell me about all the French suitors in your life."

"Oh, dear, I'm afraid it's not all that glamorous. One day Monsieur Rousse is calling on me, the next Monsieur Girard, the third it's Monsieur Martin. So many men, but not one worth thinking twice about. These French are all so passionate about everything. It gets tiring after a while." She looked to her friend. "What about you? Surely your life is brimming with interesting young bachelors as well."

Cora, with a thoughtful look, played with a tassel on one of the silk pillows.

"Well, Jonathan, my father's accountant, has been showing an interest . . . I think."

"You think?" Madeline tittered.

"My father says Jonathan is smitten by me, but I have yet to see it. It might have been he who left an apple with the maid. She said there was a blond boy calling for me, but that could have been my cousin, as well."

"Anyone else?"

"No. Unless you count my cousin."

"Well, I would think you'd have hundreds of men at your feet."

Cora frowned. Regardless of her pity, Maddy had always been the pretty one, her smile brighter, skin clearer, her bosom larger. As long as Cora had known her, she had always had men calling on her, French or otherwise. Cora knew Madeline secretly enjoyed being chased by men and probably had not yet settled down for that exact reason.

The women dressed for dinner and headed to the banquet hall. The room was adorned with tea lights, the smell of fresh pine boughs permeating the grand space.

Dinner had already begun to be served, so the girls rushed to find their seats. A full crab sat in front of them, served on fine, imported china. An attendant pulled out their seats and laid pressed linen napkins on their laps.

The noise of chatty guests around them blended with the chiming sounds of silverware against the dishes.

"Hello," *a balding gentleman sitting beside Cora said to the girls.* "I am Christopher Reed, and this is my wife Ella."

"Where are y'all from?" *Ella asked the women in an unmistakable Georgian accent. She was dressed in the colors of a peacock. On her ears hung diamonds the size of strawberries.*

"New York," *Cora said, dabbing her mouth with the napkin.*

"I can tell you're college girls," *Mr. Reed said.*

"Yes, Barnard College."

"Very nice. I read about that one," *the man said.*

A slim, young gentleman in a well-cut black dress coat with tails approached their table.

"David, dear, I want to introduce you to these lovely young ladies. I'm sorry, I didn't catch your names," *the woman said.*

"I'm Coraline Bellville and this is Madeline Van Deusen," *Cora said.*

Madeline gave the man a playful glance and extended her gloved hand. "How do you do?"

"David Reed," *the man said, gesturing to himself and giving a slight bow.* I see you've met my aunt and uncle.

David took Madeline's hand and kissed it, then moved to Cora's, his eyes set on her as he let his lips linger.

"It is a pleasure to make your acquaintence," he said.

Cora blushed.

"Miss Bellville attends Barnard College," his aunt explained.

"Is that so? I'm living in New York, as well. I am employed as a civil engineer."

"Oh, my," Madeline said, *"And what does being a civil engineer entail?"*

"Well, not to boast, but I work with the Roeblings, whose father designed the Brooklyn Bridge."

"Roeblings Bridge? I crossed over that just on Wednesday," Cora said.

"I trust it was still intact?"

"Yes, it held up marvelously," Cora said with a shy laugh. The sounds of a seven piece orchestra playing The orchestra's rendition of a newly popular tune entitled So This is Love *burst through the banquet hall.*

"Oh, I love this song," Cora said, her eyes brightening.

"Would you care to join me for this dance, Miss Bellville?" Mr. Reed asked

Cora looked back to her friend.

"I shall enjoy visiting with Mr. and Mrs. Reed," Madeline said, waving Cora on.

David offered Cora his arm, and they headed to the dance floor.

At the table, the Georgia tycoon grilled Madeline. "So what business is your father in?"

"Steel," Madeline said flatly.

"Is that so? I'm a steel man myself. Best open-hearth furnaces in Alabama. We like to keep our home back in Georgia, though. I'm sure your father's business is boomin' up north, too, eh?"

"I'm sure I wouldn't know." Madeline said, watching enviously as Cora and David glided across the floor.

When the song ended, David gave Cora a gracious bow and lead her to her table.

"Thank you, Miss Bellville. With your permission, I would like to ask you to dance again, later, as well."

"Certainly," Cora said, feeling a bit dizzy.

In their room, Cora couldn't help but rant about her dance with David.

"Who knew engineers could dance like that!"

Filing her nails, Madeline said, "He's handsome, yes, but not my type. Too rigid and formal."

"Well, he doesn't need to be your type," Cora said as she pinned her Mary Pickford curls into a loose bun, tucked her hair into her bathing cap, then pulled out her brand new swimsuit—an athletic style in navy blue jersey.

She looked to her friend who appeared to be pouting.

"Is something wrong, dear Maddy? I hope I didn't bore you, tonight," Cora said.

"Well, you did seem to spend a great deal of time with that Mr. Reed. I don't think he's good for you."

"Really? He's a New York fellow . . . with Southern charm. You can't get better than that."

"He has bad teeth." Madeline yawned.

"Oh, you're just silly," Cora said, stepping out the door to head to the loo. While Madeline was alone in the room, she pulled on her swimsuit and removed her jewelry. Unsure what to do with herself while she waited for her friend, she wandered over to Cora's suitcase and began to poke around.

It was no wonder Cora had such trouble finding men, she thought. Her clothes were so dated. But as she rummaged about, disappointed with her findings, she came across an odd little box.

Curious as to what this old thing was doing mixed with Cora's clothes, she lifted the lid only enough to reveal a red velvet liner. Just as she did, Cora returned. Madeline tossed the box back into the suitcase, appearing to be preoccupied with the bow on her suit.

"Ready to go?" Cora asked, confused by her friend's guilty look.

"Yes. Very," Madeline said.

The girls slipped on their Kimono-style robes and walked down the halls, found the stairs, and made their way to the basement floor.

The air was humid and thick, even more than it was outside. As they walked beneath an archway, they entered a large room with a vaulted ceiling. In the center was a magnificent one-hundred-twenty-foot-long swimming pool. Potted tropical plants lined the perimeter, and Japanese lanterns hung overhead from three stories above. A man on a swing, suspended twenty feet up, readied himself before plummeting into the water

Above the pool were two floors of arched balconies. Partygoers in their lavish New Year's attire gazed over the railings, amused by the swimmer's antics.

Cora and Madeline looked around in awe while draping their robes over wicker poolside furnishings then made their way down the marble stairs, submersing themselves waist high in the cool water. A beach ball landed in front of Cora, splashing her face. A tall man from the crowd leapt forward to retrieve it.

"I'm sorry, miss. Our game is getting a bit rowdy," he said. When he recognized the girls he smiled. "Well, hello, Miss Bellville," David said, wet hair in his eyes.

"Oh, hello!" Cora said.

"This pool is just marvelous, isn't it?" Madeline said, interrupting their moment. "Such a wonderful way to bring in the New Year, wouldn't you say?" she asked, eyeing David with a flirtatious grin.

David turned back to Cora.

"Would you like to try the swing?"

"Oh no," Cora answered "I can't swim. Besides, I like to keep my feet on the ground."

"So, does that mean you have no interest in being swept off your feet?"

Cora blushed.

A man in a striped suit and a well-trimmed mustache dove into the water from the side of the pool, causing a rippling of waves.

"Would you like to sit along the side where it is a bit less raucous?," David asked, offering Cora his arm.

Madeline frowned, following behind as they stepped out of the water.

"So, Cora what do you study at Barnard?" David asked.

"English Literature."

"So, I take it you're a devotee of the classics?"

"Yes. Shakespeare, in particular!"

"Ah. Romeo and Juliette," David said, his voice softening.

Madeline rolled her eyes, then in another attempt to gain David's attention she spoke, "You know, I spent a whole week in Verona, where Romeo and Juliette took place. I even visited the tomb fabled to be the setting for their suicides."

David looked to Madeline and with a teasing smile said, "Romeo and Juliette committed suicide? The atrocity." He turned to Cora and laughed.

"Oh, Maddie, it seems you've ruined the ending for poor Mr. Reed."

Madeline, for the first time the odd one out, was not faring well.

Needing to separate herself from Cora and the annoying man, she decided to go for a swim. Though a young lady swimming off in a crowded pool by herself was not quite socially acceptable, Maddie didn't care. She needed to get away from those two, clear her head.

All around her, people played, splashing and shouting, an echoing of revelry that seemed to mock Madeline's lonely state.

She watched longingly as couples three stories up, dressed in tuxedos and extravagant evening dresses, laughed with one another. All at once, she noticed a dark silhouette apart from the crowd. It appeared to sit on the ledge, precariously perched like a crow, its shape like shifting smoke. Madeline headed back to the couple and spoke with excitement.

"Look! Look! Look at that creature up there. Do you see it?" she pointed three stories up.

Cora looked in the direction of her finger and smiled.

"The woman in purple?"

"No. The shadow, sitting on the ledge."

A wild laughter echoed through the hotel in sharp contrast to all the jovial voices in the ballroom. It echoed not just in the room, but within her.

David turned to Cora, and the two chuckled.

"I think someone must have slipped something into your friend's punch tonight," he said.

"No. It's there," Madeline said. *"Come with me. We'll go up and see it."* She pulled her arm.

"In our swimsuits? Are you daft?" Cora asked incredulously. *"It's just about midnight. Come over to the cabana and get some champagne."*

Madeline was on a mission. She climbed out of the pool and headed to the stairs, her woolen jersey suit heavy with water.

A woman in a red dress backed out of her way when she saw the wet, swimsuited girl heading in her direction. Madeline was oblivious. She continued on to the next level, leaving a trail of puddles across the smooth marble floors.

When she reached the spot where the shadow had sat, it was gone. Madeline looked over the rail to find her friend and the man still talking, but now, hovering beside them was that dark creature who just moments before was there.

"Hey! Hey!" she called, waving her arms wildly trying to attract her friend's attention.

David looked up and directed Cora's gaze to Madeline. Cora glanced at her briefly then turned away, pretending not to see her.

Furious, Madeline ran down the stairs as fast as she could without slipping. A trail of water remained behind her. When she got to the pool, she approached Cora.

"Cora, please tell me you can see that dark spirit beside you. It's there!"

"Madeline, I really think you need to control yourself," she whispered. She turned to David and excused herself. She led her friend to an isolated spot in the pool.

"Maddy, I remember you being the boisterous one at school, but this is absurd. I never recall you going to such extremes for attention."

Madeline ignored her, keeping her eye on the shadow that hovered near David, who was sitting alone while watching a group of men dive from the board.

"I don't know what appropriate behavior in France is, but what you're doing is certainly not appropriate here. I think it would serve you well to come back with me to the room."

Madeline didn't respond.

"Mr. Reed has asked me to go on a walk through the gardens with him later this evening. Alone. You're my closest friend in the world; please tell me you have your wits about you enough to council me on this matter. Shall I go with him?"

Madeline didn't hear Cora. She was focused solely on the strange laughter that surrounded her.

Cora continued. "I hope there are no hard feelings tonight. I don't mean to be ignoring you. I just really like this David fellow . . . and frankly I'm dumbfounded that it's me rather than you getting lavished with attention. Maybe the tides are turning, eh?"

With Cora's words, the laughter in Madeline's head deepened and echoed floor to ceiling across the entire hall. It was the clearest, most distinct sound Madeline had ever heard, and in that moment it spoke to her. She knew what she had to do.

As midnight approached and the revelers began their count down,

"10 . . . 9 . . . 8 . . ."

Madeline, unconcerned with the festivities, took Cora's hands in hers, and smiled. Cora looked at her, confused.

"7 . . . 6 . . . 5 . . . 4 . . ."

With more strength than she knew, Madeline tugged on Cora's arm, dragging her friend down deep beneath the water. Madeline stood solid with her torso above the water, a devilish smile on her face, while her friend struggled. In spite of Cora's thrashing, Madeline kept herself steady, unyielding, until her friend's struggle was just a ripple in the commotion of the night.

"3 . . . 2 . . . 1 . . ."

As the crowd's cheers echoed through the hall, Cora's lifeless body sank to the bottom.

Madeline walked from the water slow and steady, unperturbed.

She tucked some stray strands of hair back under her bathing cap, turned to David and said, "Cora has turned in early for the night. She's not feeling well."

"But she didn't even say good bye," he said, looking dejected.

"Women are fickle that way." She gave him a wide smile and headed for the stairs.

Chapter 29

Now free of Brad and that stuffy shop, Olivia pirouetted down the dark street, her flip flops tossed somewhere along the way, allowing her bare toes now to savor the smooth concrete.

It was bar time on a Monday night, and college students poured from the taverns. Olivia passed a group of girls, all probably from New York and New Jersey, wearing their "going out" attire: high heels, big earrings that dangled to their shoulders, and tops that showed their cleavage. They eyed her with disapproval as she skipped alone across the street, humming to herself.

Almost to spite them, Olivia pulled off her shirt, spun it over her head, and tossed it into a nearby tree. A few boys walking past cheered. She smiled devilishly.

Brad dragged himself out of the store and tried to catch up with Olivia. He heard a series of hoots and hollers and looked to see Olivia in her bra dancing like a bad Las Vegas stripper for several boys. Brad watched her dance under the street lights, the shadow like a loyal dog keeping at her feet.

Olivia made her way down the street, farther from the crowds, until only a few revelers remained. King Street was completely quiet. Even the usual hum of bugs in the park was absent. The silence was too much for Olivia. She needed stimulation to stay satisfied. She needed sights, sounds, actions. Guided solely by her animal impulses, she headed west.

In front of Olivia, Flagler College loomed dark, like a forbidden castle. Across the street was another building. This one in pink stone, accentuated by two, six-story pillars. Formerly the lavish Alcazar Hotel, the building now housed the Lightner Museum, hosting a large collection of art and oddities from the late 19th century.

Olivia knew this building well. She had visited it often during her time as a student. Renaissance Revival was her thing, but now she wasn't thinking about term papers or classroom syllabi. In fact, she wasn't thinking much at all.

The moon, on the verge of full, poured opalescent light onto her features, causing her to glow like a celestial being. In her primitive-like state, she scampered down the passageway into a courtyard open to the sky. In the center, up above, tiny stars pierced through the blackness.

Olivia followed a stone bridge over a pond of sleeping koi. She leaned over the edge, reached down, dipped her hand in the water, and stirred it with her fingers. Several of the larger fish roused, swam to the surface, and kissed her hand.

Then, motivated by wild curiosity, Olivia rose and wandered down the outside corridor until she reached a door adorned with stained glass, a winged angel as its centerpiece. Captivated, she let her hand glide against smoothness of the glass, carefully tracing the leaded lines with her fingers.

With a sudden urge to enter the building, she yanked on the door handle, but it didn't move. Then, after pulling several more times, she scanned the area. Her eye landed on a pile of bricks being used for a current restoration project. She lifted one, drew her arm back, and with a strong throw tossed it at the door. Magnificent shards of green, blue, and yellow glass fell to the ground like confetti, scattering across the marble floor. In the distance of her mind came a noise. At first it struck her as a baby's cry, some far off child in distress, then it evolved into something more eerie, like a lone wolf howling to its pack.

Above the wail, she heard a man shout. She turned to see a heavyset man in a white oxford shirt and black pants, with keys hanging from his belt, lumbering towards her.

"Stop!" he yelled, the keys jingling as he ran.

All she knew in that moment was that she wasn't going to let this man spoil her fun.

She reached her hand through the freshly made hole and unlocked the door, letting herself in. Still her eager companion, the shadow followed close behind.

Stepping barefoot like a seasoned firewalker on hot coals she walked indifferently through the shattered glass then took off through the museum. Olivia passed the tall pillars of the grand entryway, hopped over the turnstyle, and climbed a series of stairs two at a time until she reached level three of the ballroom. There, an expansive balcony wrapped around a large central space that looked three floors down to a beautifully tiled café, once the space for a grand swimming pool.

The sirens howled through the building, but Olivia was unaware of their call. Instead she was captivated by the hand-carved chairs adorned for long-gone emperors. On a Grecian pedestal beside them stood a winged woman in white porcelain reaching down to touch the cheek of an earthbound man. Olivia, unconcerned with museum rules, picked it up and turned it in her hands, bringing her fingertip to meet the angel's extended hand as if she had a connection with this girl.

The chattering of a walkie talkie came from the stairs.

She could make out a man's words, "Caucasian female. Black bra."

Out of breath, the guard said, "I'm headed to the third-floor mezzanine."

Olivia placed the sculpture on the ground. Like a child pursued in a game of tag, she ran with glee, descending a stairway, completely unaware of the pain of the glass now embedded deep within her feet.

Without windows to let the moonlight in, the downstairs was dark, except for the red glow of the exit signs that gave the walls a warm, velvety texture. Along the perimeter hung portraits of merchants' daughters, stiff-collared kings, and silver-suited generals. In the center, on wooden pedestals, sat several cloisonné helmets in gold and blues. She looked at them briefly, until she was drawn with an almost magnetic force to something in the corner.

She approached the object slowly, her breath still heavy from her run. On a platform stood a small, worn box, covered in ornately carved flowers.

She moved towards it cautiously and reached out her hands. She cupped it gently and brought it in close. Beneath the soft red light she read the words, *non plus chaos*. It was almost identical to the one she had left at the Phoenix.

She needed this box. There was no doubt. It was meant for her.

The elevator opened, and two police officers appeared, their hands on their guns. Olivia clutched the box under her arm and fled the room. Running up a flight of stairs, she pushed the emergency exit open and escaped into the silence of the street.

She ran down the narrow streets, weaving through back alleys, unconscious of her movements until she found herself at the front step of Brad's tattoo shop.

She pounded on the door.

"Brad!" she yelled.

When no one answered, she cupped her hand over her eyes and peered into the shop. Seeing no one, she knocked again.

"You looking for someone?" a voice spoke. Olivia turned to see Brad, obscured by the darkness of the street, leaning on the building, a cigarette in hand. He exhaled a stream of smoke, his eyes dazed as if he had just woken from sleep.

She turned to him and her face lit with wild intensity.

"Brad, I have something for you . . . something wonderful!"

"Liv? Where have you been?"

She thought for a moment. Even though she knew she had just been somewhere important, she couldn't remember where it was.

"I don't know, actually. But I do know I got a gift for you while I was out." She pulled the box from behind her back.

Brad squinted. "What is it?"

"It's another one."

"What do you mean *another one*?"

"I mean there's more. And I don't think there's just these two. I think there are lots of them."

Brad took it in his hands and inspected it.

"Where did you find it?"

"I have no clue."

He furrowed his brow. Olivia ignored his displeased reaction.

"Brad, do you realize what this means? We're not alone. Who knows how many boxes could be out there. How many shadows? Just think, there are other people in this town, maybe all over the world, who are going through the same thing we are."

She looked at him with loving eyes. "I think this box is what you need. Maybe this is a better shadow. I mean, maybe it will open you up like the other one does for me."

Brad's face hardened. "I think I'm opened enough, thank you."

Olivia laughed out loud. "Oh, really? I beg to differ. Brad, come on. You're missing out. I want you feel the shadow like I do and share with me in this wonderfulness."

"Yeah? At what cost?"

"Whatever the cost, it's no greater than the cost of living your life blind." Olivia stilled and gave him a serious look. "I don't know if you see it, but all of this is happening for a reason," Olivia said. "The box, the shadow . . . the osprey!"

"Maybe so, but I think that the reason is to cause me pain. This shadow thrives on my suffering. And it's feeding off *your* disorder." He gestured to the shadow. "Don't you see? It's growing? Living off our deterioration?"

"I don't care. I think we should open it," Olivia said, her eyes wide with excitement.

"You're fucking crazy!"

"Yes, I am. I'm alive. If the shadow wasn't burdening you with fear, you'd be all for opening it, too."

"No, I wouldn't. I've lost too much in my life. There's no room for losing more."

"Yes! Exactly. Isn't that it?" Olivia's eyes grew wild. "Now that we are stripped of our former selves, there's nothing left to hold us back—we can be free."

"If this is freedom, I don't want any part of it." Brad tossed his cigarette to the ground and crushed it with the heel of his boot. He continued. "I don't think you see yourself right now. You're like a barefoot savage. You may feel free, but from my vantage point you look like a crazy woman."

Dark laughter bounced off the walls of the shops, and the shadow rose.

A sly smile grew on Olivia's face and she felt the wildness growing within her again.

"You know what? Fuck you," she said and brought her hand to the clasp and unhooked it. She lifted the lid.

Instantly, the sounds of a woman's laughter filled the air as a slender shadow snaked its way out, like a cobra charmed by its master. The new creature slithered its way towards the original shadow, and then, as if in a happy reunion dance, they spiraled around each other.

In a dizzying motion, the two spirits twisted and rose, hovering at the tree tops. Brad and Olivia watched with terror and fascination as the mass of swirling greys and blacks moved like a living storm dominating the narrow street.

Olivia felt a new lightness, as if her body was so buoyant, so inflated that her toes barely touched the ground. Her eyes grew with desire, her body hungry for disarray, and she moved towards Brad, wrapping her hands behind his neck and pulling his face right up to hers. "I want you so bad, biker man," she purred. "We are meant for each other. Now."

In a fury Brad gave her a shove. "You idiot!" he bellowed as she caught herself from falling.

The box tumbled to the ground, lying open on its side.

"You have no idea what you've done," he said as he grabbed the box from the street to keep it out of her reach and shouted, "Leave!"

A look of hurt flashed on her face for just a brief moment, but as quickly as it came it was replaced with a manic smile.

"Gladly," she said, and she turned down the street with a skip in her step.

Chapter 30

Brad was wandering through the ancient passageways of a deteriorating city. Olivia was with him, sometimes leading, sometimes following. Together they sought something, but what, exactly, neither was sure. After exploring many narrow passageways in the town, they came to the center of a labyrinth.

In front of them was a pool of luminescent liquid, glowing with a rippling light that reflected on Olivia's bright skin. Olivia, uninhibited, moved to the edge, dipped her hand in the water and pulled out a large glowing pearl. She smiled, recognizing the object. This was what they had been looking for, but just as she reached out to share the gift with him, darkness slid across Brad's vision, obscuring both Olivia and the pearl. As a blackness fell upon him, Brad yelled out to her. He woke to the sound of his own voice.

When he awoke, Brad found himself lying atop his unmade bed, sheets twisted all around him. In the still of the morning, he let his heart settle, reminding himself it was just a dream. As his mind quieted, things were okay. Dog was not sick. Shadows didn't chase him and boxes hadn't been opened. His life was a pleasant collection of ordinary events, like it had been for years. But this fragile illusion held itself only for a moment. Just the act of rolling to one side brought him back to his misery.

Brad felt the weight of the shadow, his friend's illness, and the mystery of the strange new woman in his life. His body hurt.

He moaned and rubbed his eyes. Moving slowly, he sat up and noticed in the far corner of his room the narrow female shadow was hovering against the wall, as if it had been watching him all night.

"God fucking damn it," he muttered, turning over and pulling the blanket over his head.

A few moments later he felt a nudge. Brad jumped.

His white pit bull, with his tail wagging wildly, was ready to start the day.

"Okay. Okay," Brad said, and he rose and slipped on a pair of boxers and shorts, trying to ignore the shadow.

He started the coffee, made his ritual breakfast of toast and a fried egg, and then let Ghost out the back door, watching through the screen as his dog sniffed around the edges of the fenced-in yard. Brad ate his breakfast in silence.

There was a knock on the door.

Outside, in a black tank top and short shorts, stood Cheri from Scarlett O'Hara's. He always welcomed her drop-in visits, but now he noticed that right beside her was the female shadow, as if it was bringing him the girl as some kind of offering.

"Hey, Brad. Sorry to bug you," she said. "I was in the area and just thought I'd stop by. Can I come in?"

Ghost stuck his nose between the door jam and Brad's leg. Cheri leaned down and let him sniff her hand.

"Hey, poochy-woochie. I missed you!" she said.

Ghost shook his tail with such fervor that his whole backside shook.

Brad tucked his hair behind his ears. "I was actually heading to the shop early."

"Oh, okay, no problem . . . You seemed distracted Friday night. What's been bugging you?"

"Nothing. Nothing at all," he lied.

Brad's phone rang from the kitchen.

"I gotta grab that," he said, leaving Cheri, the shadow, and rambunctious Ghost at the open door.

He answered. It was Suze.

"Hey Suzy-Q!" he said, pretending as if both their lives weren't falling apart.

"Brad, where have you been? Dog's asking for you."

"I've just been swamped at the shop. I'm sorry. I'll come by later. I promise."

"Come now. Dog is going into surgery again." Her voice got weak. "They're opening up his chest this time, Brad."

He hesitated. "Well, I've got someone here, right now…"

"Brad, what the hell is with you? You need to get some balls. This is serious shit. Your friend is going into open-heart surgery and you're pussying around?"

"I know. I know. I'll be there soon," he said as he hung up.

Rather than leaving, as Brad had hoped, Cheri had let herself in and was sitting on his couch looking around at the pictures on his walls. The shadow sat beside her on one side while Ghost was on the other, nudging his big head into her lap.

"Hey, uh . . ." he said, running his hands through his unbrushed hair and wondering what the hell he was going to do with her.

She gave him an alluring smile, "I was thinking, since I'm here anyway, ya wanna fuck? You know, for old time's sake."

The slender shadow laughed, pleased with this perfect gift she had brought him.

Chapter 31

When Olivia woke Wednesday morning, her head was resting in an awkward position, a set of stairs jutting into her ribs and hip. She looked up and saw a crooked banister and two spindles knocked out of place, and she knew she was outside her apartment, resting on the stairs.

Apparently, she had found her way back on the previous night but had never actually made it inside. Olivia shifted, feeling a soreness in her hip and neck where the stairs met her body. She looked down and noticed she was in just a bra and a skirt. Panicked, she searched for her purse so she could get her keys and her phone but didn't see it.

Thinking back to the previous night, she tried to remember when she had had it last. She could recall the ride to the Fairchild

Oak, the kiss in the branches, sitting with Brad at his shop discussing tattoos, but after that it got hazy.

A door opened at the base of her stairs, and her neighbor, Mary Ellen, emerged in a nightgown with a bag of trash in her hand. She eyed Olivia up and down and gave her a look of concern.

Olivia looked away, embarrassed. The wail of a distant ambulance came into her awareness and a fuzzy memory emerged of the previous night: a blaring siren calling out in the night as she ran, and she knew she had been part of some bizarre game of chase.

Hoping to shake this dream, she stood and steadied herself against the wall. As she placed her bare feet on the steps, she noticed a sharp piercing pain that started at her feet and traveled up her leg. Lifting a foot, she found shards of colored glass in reds, blues, greens, embedded deep in the skin. Splotches of dried blood coated the cuts in a brown, muddled mess, while red-brown smears dotted the steps below.

In a flash it came to her, the joy of watching glass shatter and the thrill of fleeing from an unseen foe. Though it wasn't all clear, whatever she had done wasn't good. She was pretty sure of that.

She sat back down and plucked a green shard from her big toe and, as she watched a bead of blood emerge from the skin, she wished to herself that the act of removing glass had the power to eliminate her previous night's sins.

Stepping on the sides of her feet to avoid any more pain, she climbed the stairs and took a spare key from beneath the mat and unlocked her door. The oven clock said ten thirty. She was already three and a half hours late for work.

Olivia went into her bathroom, unhooked her bra, splashed water on her face, and then grabbed a clean black camisole and a pair of jean shorts. In the mirror, with no shadow to influence her, Olivia was not the bright, seductive goddess she knew just yesterday. She was worn, haggard, and drained—just an empty vessel waiting to be filled.

After cleaning herself up, she walked to the front door. With her flip flops nowhere in sight, she grabbed a pair of socks and tennis shoes. Welcoming the soft, protective cotton on her feet, she slipped on her shoes and headed to the bakery.

Olivia walked into town detached from all the sights and sounds that had entranced her just the day before. In fact, without the shadow near her, her body had once again returned to a state of apathy.

As she walked towards Kernel Poppers Popcorn Shop, she noticed one of her flip flops lying upside down by the base of a palm tree, the other tossed into a potted plant. Beside the tree, stood the male shadow, as if it had been waiting for her all along. In a strange greeting, it let out a lingering laugh.

Olivia approached it. Up close it was not just an absence of light but a swirling mass of blacks and greys, a storm within itself. Uninhibited and hungry for its power, she brought her hand right up to the dark being and pushed forward until her fingers slipped past the shadow's boundaries into its darkness. To Olivia's surprise, there was no sensation at all, not hot, not cold, not smooth, nor coarse. It was as if the shadow in all its potency wasn't real at all, just a vision, a hallucination that she and Brad shared.

Yet, as illusionary as it may have been, Olivia was not immune. In the instant after touching the creature, she once again felt ravenous. Now infused with power, a broad smile pulled across her face and she continued towards Eat It Too.

From outside the shop, she could see Mandie in the window, placing cupcakes in the case, with a melancholy air. On any other day, Olivia would have run into the shop and apologized profusely, but not now with the shadow on her side. She felt hot, ready for a fight.

Olivia stepped in.

Mandie glanced up for a moment and muttered, "It's about time," then moved into the back room.

Olivia followed, the shadow trailing along.

"You gonna talk to me?" she asked.

Mandie remained silent, turning her back.

"Come on. I know I'm late. Isn't that enough to send you into a mother fucking tizzy?" Olivia asked.

Mandie looked at her, exhausted. "Olivia, what has happened to you? This can't work like this, with you all crazy and irresponsible. I need you to be solid. The shop can't function with you falling apart. I want the old you back."

Power surged within Olivia like storm clouds on the edge of a front.

"The old me is gone."

Mandie turned her back again and began sweeping ferociously.

Olivia piped up. "So, it's okay for you to not show up in the morning, forget orders, not pay the bills? But me? If I don't show up for work for one God damned morning, it's the end of the world?"

"Olivia, we had a good thing going. I'm the creative one, you're the orderly, meticulous one. It's worked for five years. Why are you fucking it up now?"

"You think I liked being your fucking cleanup crew all these years?" Olivia felt like fire came from her eyes. "I mean, hell, what about Sunday night? Fucking your boyfriend in the shop and leaving the mess for me? That is okay?!"

"What the hell are you talking about?" Mandie asked.

"Monday morning, I came in here. You had left the door unlocked, the music going, and a God damned *ass* print on the counter. You fucked Tank right in our kitchen."

"I did not! I would never," Mandie shrieked. "How could you even think I'd do something so shitty? Besides, I left before you."

"No, I left first," Olivia said.

"Don't tell me you don't remember!" Mandie yelled.

Olivia frowned.

"Just as we were about to leave, you started sending texts to God knows who. You muttered something about a booty call and told me to leave."

Olivia's face went white.

"Who'd I call?"

"I don't know, but some nasty guy with shoulder-length blond hair came in here earlier today and left these," Mandie said, pulling out a pair of black panties from beneath the counter.

Olivia was smacked with the truth. She saw it all: her skirt hiked up, her bare butt on the cold counter as a man she barely knew pounded into her, a ridiculous grin on his face.

She grabbed the underwear from Mandie's hand and stuffed them in her pocket.

Mandie sneered. "The guy said to me, 'That friend of yours gives great head. Tell her I'm ready for another go around,' . . . or something like that. I had no idea what he was talking about, nor did I want to."

Mandie looked to her friend with sad eyes. "Olivia, what's happening to you? Do you no longer care about the shop? Or us? Or yourself? Screwing disgusting guys right in our kitchen? Leaving the store unlocked, then blaming me?"

Olivia didn't answer. She just watched her friend's lips as they spat out angry words.

"Don't you have anything to say for yourself?"

Olivia felt the anger rise, but this time it wasn't directed at Mandie, but herself.

When Olivia looked at her without emotion, Mandie shouted, "You're a bullshit friend, you know that?" Tears ran down her cheeks. "Get out of this God damned place, you irresponsible whore."

Mandie's words hit Olivia like a punch to the face. Unable to process the onslaught of anger and shame, she turned and ran out the door.

Chapter 32

Brad really wanted—no, needed—a quick lay, and Cheri, the little spitfire, was ready and rearing. But with the shadow looming close by, he was afraid of where it might lead.

"Look, I would love to," he said, ". . . but, I can't. I've got some stuff going on that I need to deal with."

"Then a quickie! Fifteen minutes? I promise. Just *Wham bam, thank you, ma'am,* then I'm out the door."

Nerves on edge, Brad looked to the shadow.

"I really, really should go," he said, but Cheri ignored his words and moved in closer.

"Come on," she said, looking pleased with the package in his pants. She slowly unbuttoned his shorts and lowered herself to her knees.

She pulled down his zipper, worked her hand into his boxers and wrapped her fingers around his still-soft cock.

She played with it, enticing it.

When he still didn't respond, she placed her lips tight around it and let her tongue dance on the tip. Still no reaction.

Brad brought his fingers through her hair and closed his eyes, trying to let all thoughts of Dog, the shadow, and Olivia fade away. He needed this. He deserved this.

He felt her coaxing, her heated effort to get him to rise, but nothing worked. Brad opened his eyes and looked down at her. She returned his glance with disappointment.

"I suppose when guys get to be your age they have trouble getting it up."

The female shadow laughed savagely. Brad pulled away, feeling dark bile rise within him. His energy ran to his hands, to his feet, and he yelled, "Get the fuck out of my house." The girl gave him a terrified look and ran out the door.

Fueled with rage from his shadow's manipulation, Brad ran through the house, looking for his keys. He tossed about a pile of jeans discarded on the floor of his room and threw aside the bed sheets hoping the keys would appear. With rabid passion, in the kitchen he sent a stack of mail flying off the counter, causing Ghost to run away in fear.

"Fuck!" he screamed.

The keys, as if teasing him, sat on the banister next to the door. He grabbed them and ran to his bike, the shadow following behind.

Brad reached the hospital, feeling a cocktail of emotions boiling in his blood. The long, tiled corridors seemed to close in on him as he ran. At the elevator, a man in a wheelchair with a tank of oxygen in tow sat with his wife, coughing as he waited. Each cough from this man made Brad wince in agony, as if his lungs, too, were filled with phlegm. The pain was too much. Agony bled from the walls, seeping into his bones. He found the stairs and climbed the five flights up.

On Dog's floor, the halls were almost silent, marked only by the staccato beats of Brad's livid heart. Nurses worked at computers while a doctor read over a patient's chart. Brad walked all the way to Dog's room at the end of the hall, now out of breath.

The room was empty. The bed was made and his belongings were packed away into a large plastic bag and left by the door.

Frantic, Brad returned to the nurse's station.

"Where's my friend?"

The nurse in orange Garfield scrubs eyed Brad up and down and gestured to one of the male nurses to handle him.

"It's all okay, sir. Calm down. Who is your friend?"

"Robert Struthers."

The man looked to the other nurses and returned his gaze to Brad. "I'm sorry . . . HIPAA regulations forbid me to speak with you about anything concerning Mr. Struthers. Why don't you have a seat and wait for his wife. She's coming by to pick up his belongings."

"Wait, why?" Brad asked with panic in his voice. "Is he being transferred to another floor?"

"Just have a seat," one of the female nurses said, "Mrs. Struthers will be here shortly." She put a hand on his shoulder and directed him towards a chair.

"No!" Brad turned to her with a wild look in his eye. "I demand to see him, now."

"I'm sorry. That is not a choice, sir." The woman said, speaking to him like he was four years old. "Please sit down."

"I will not. Not until you tell me what's really going on here."

"Sir, sit." The nurse said again.

"All right, just tell me this, and I will. Is Dog—Robert Struthers—all right?"

The nurse bowed her head, biting her top lip as if in an effort to keep the truth sealed away.

"What? Tell me!" He said, his voice wavering.

"I'm sorry. We cannot disclose that information at this time."

Brad looked to the other female nurse behind the station, hoping she would tell him more. She just remained by the computer, her fingers still on the keys, pretending the current drama in the ICU was of no concern, but her look of pity said it all. Dog was dead. Brad was sure.

Brad heard a chuckle and turned around to see the shadow, standing behind him.

"You did this! You killed Dog, you mother fucker!" Brad yelled.

The shadow continued laughing as if amused to no end by his suffering.

"Get the hell away from me, you demon!" Brad thrashed at the air in a feeble attempt to rid himself of the shadow.

The nurses looked at each other and nodded in agreement, and the male nurse grabbed the phone and placed a call.

He hung it up then stepped forward and put his hand on Brad's shoulder. Brad pushed it away.

"Someone's going to be here shortly to help you."

"I don't need *help*. I need this God damned shadow gone."

The shadow laughed again, and Brad began to feel woozy, as if his insides were dissolving within his body. He tried desperately to hold onto his sense of control, but he was helpless. He fell to the floor.

Brad stood in his childhood living room. A green, floral-print couch sat against the wall on an orange shag carpet. He had just arrived home from middle school, feeling rowdy from the games his friends and he had played on the way home. In contrast to his playful demeanor, the house was quiet, with no signs of his brother or mom.

The screen door slammed behind him and he walked into the living room.

"Ma, I'm home!" he called.

He saw his mom, but she wasn't in her normal spot, listening to her favorite radio show. Instead she was lying on the rug, her arm twisted at an uncomfortable angle. He stepped closer and saw bruises wrapped like macabre jewelry in greens and purple around her neck.

"Mom?"

When she didn't respond, he gave her a tap, hoping to wake her. Not only did she not move, her body was stiff.

"Mom," he said, more panicked, tapping her with more and more force to get her to wake. But nothing worked. He ran for the phone and dialed the ambulance.

He spoke to dispatch: "I can't wake my mom up," he said, and then described the bruises up and down her body.

OPEN SOULS

Waiting for the ambulance Brad sat by her side, patting her back gently, saying "Help is coming soon, don't worry, Mom. They'll be here soon. You're going to be fine."

The paramedics arrived with several police cars. Two officers with no-nonsense looks ushered Brad into the kitchen. They had questions.

Brad told them everything; about the bars where his dad hung out, the types of jobs he held, but most importantly he told them about the years of violence his mother had endured. His father was an angry man. Everyone knew it in their small Iowa town. No one would be surprised.

Several days later, at his mother's graveside, the bare trees with their spindly frames stood black against the November sky. The cold midwestern air blew across the neighboring corn fields and into the cemetery, causing several grieving friends to shudder, but Brad didn't feel it. His skin—his whole body—was numb.

The casket was lowered slowly into the grave, and the sobs of women he didn't even know echoed off the grey skies. He looked across the gravesite and with a taciturn gaze looked at the man responsible for all this. In spite of the evidence against him, Brad's father was a smooth talker with friends at the police station. He wouldn't be indicted for many years to come.

Brad's father looked at his son and smiled wide. Brad felt the anger churn in his gut, but pushed it down. He would not be like his dad. Ever. He would always be in control.

As the reverend spoke, the smell of freshly dug dirt tunneled into Brad's consciousness, creating a wound so deep it would forever trigger the sick feeling of death in him.

Brad woke in a hospital bed still smelling dirt, his body curled into itself, the pillow wet from tears. A balding man with wire glasses sat beside him holding a clipboard and talking in a soft voice with Suze, who stood over him looking ashen and drained.

Brad looked around and sat up slowly.

"Where am I?" he asked.

"You're in the hospital. Everything is fine, Mr. Marlow. Just sit back and relax. I'm Dr. Stampen, the psychiatrist on duty tonight. You appear to have had a psychotic break."

Brad laughed. "Is that so?" he said sarcastically, sitting up straighter.

"Stress can sometimes do this, but with a little medication we can get you on track, again." Without another word, he began writing on a prescription pad. "What's your date of birth?"

Brad ignored him and looked at Suze.

She broke into tears. Brad rose from the bed, went over, wrapped himself around her, and they embraced in their shared loss.

Suze pulled away and looked at Brad.

"What happened? I thought he was going in for surgery," he said.

"Dog left for the operating room not long after you and I talked. They started working on him, but he didn't make it even fifteen minutes in. He died on the operating table." Suze's lip quivered. "I need you to be strong for me, Brad. I can't have you falling apart, okay?"

"Of course," Brad said, trying to believe his own words.

The doctor cleared his throat, interrupting their embrace. "Grieving is a process," he said. "Lives change. Healing will take time. Crying is okay."

"Thanks for the tips, doc." Brad said, although his attempt at humor was lost to the sadness of the room.

Brad looked at Suze. "Let's get out of here."

The doctor piped up, "Actually, you will have to wait here. You will need a nurse to discharge you."

"I don't think so," Brad said, and he took Suze's hand and headed down the stairs.

Chapter 33

In a wild panic, Olivia ran to the Phoenix. She tugged on the door handle, and then pounded on the glass, but no one answered.

"Brad, Brad. Please answer," she sobbed. "I think I've really fucked up." When he didn't answer, she dropped onto the front step and placed her head in her hands.

"Well, well, well, if it isn't little Olive."

Olivia looked up to see Buzz with a snake-like grin on his face.

Olivia felt herself darken with shame. This unkempt man, with the greasy hair and nicotine-stained fingers was certainly not the sort of man that would land on her candidates' list for a one night stand.

Beside him was a girl, watching their interaction with smoldering distrust. Her face was drained, her eyes red as if she'd been crying for days.

She approached Olivia, looking down on her as if disgusted with Olivia's presence.

"This is Olivia. She owns that decked-out cupcake shop down the street," Buzz said. "She even gave me the *full tour*." He looked at Olivia and raised his eyebrows.

Olivia felt her stomach churn.

The girl turned to Buzz, "What the fuck? Why haven't you ever mentioned her to me?"

"Why? Are you jealous?" Buzz jabbed.

"Are you really flaunting some whore-bitch at me? I can't handle this, now," The girl pulled out a key, unlocked the door, and stepped inside the darkened shop.

Buzz followed after her and turned to Olivia, who stood on the street looking overwhelmed.

"Come on in," he said licking his lips. "Maybe we can get a little ménage action going on."

Courtney in anger shoved a wheeled chair across the room. The three of them watched as it hit the back wall and crashed over.

"What's up your ass? I thought we decided the other day that we were going to do the open-relationship thing."

Courtney let out a shriek and headed to the back room. Sobs could be heard coming through the door.

Buzz was instantly on Olivia. "You were such a good fuck, girl. Damn, the way you howled. I mean, flour everywhere. You were like some kind of cake-baking animal." He brought his hips right up to her waist and grinded a few times against her. "Let's do it again, pretty mama."

Olivia stepped back, feeling complete disgust towards him and hatred at herself for not even being able to remember what she had done. She walked to the front counter, found her purse, and checked to see the boxes were still there.

Concealing them, she looked at Buzz. "I actually came here to see Brad."

"Why? For a tattoo?"

"Uh," She thought for a moment. "Yeah. We're working on something."

"You got a picture?"

"Yeah," Olivia showed him her arm.

"Pretty nice stencil," he said. "Tell you what, it looks like you're all ready to do this, but the old man is sort of out of commission. I can do it."

"What happened?" Olivia asked with concern.

"Aw, some shit, you know. His best friend died." He looked at her arm. "So how about it? I can get it looking real nice."

Olivia frowned and spoke, "Well . . . he and I sort of have this thing going."

"A *thing*, huh?"

Olivia nodded.

"You know Brad's a mega man-slut, don't you?"

"I guess I sort of heard that. But not the extent . . ." Olivia said, prompting him for more.

"Oh, yeah, he'll pretty much fuck whatever moves. Old ladies, fat chicks, married women . . ."

Olivia gave him a confused look.

"Yeah, he fucked my girl, too. Ass wipe."

More crying came through from the walls of the other room, and Olivia looked to Buzz hoping he would go help her, but he kept on talking.

"She's fine. Grieving and shit . . . but, yeah, about Brad; don't get too attached to him. He tosses women out like trash on the curb. Don't fool yourself, he's in it for himself," he said, grabbing a stool.

"Come here," He tapped the seat.

Olivia, feeling numb, sat down. He turned on a light at Brad's station then pulled her wrist forward. "Let's see what we can do."

Chapter 34

Brad took Suze to her sister's house, stepped off the motorcycle, and gave her a lingering hug, promising he would be there for her from now on.

After saying his goodbyes, he headed to the shop. The lights were on at the Phoenix. He figured Courtney was there to get things in order.

Expecting only her, he was surprised to find Buzz at his station inspecting the stencil on Olivia's arm.

Brad shouted, "What the hell are you doing?"

Olivia stood up. Before she could speak, he looked at Buzz. "Get out of my shop—Now!" He glared, ready for a fight.

Buzz rose from his chair and stumbled backward.

"If I ever see your little rat face again in this shop, I *will* kill you," he said pointing his finger at Buzz's face.

Brad walked towards Olivia, fuming.

"What the hell did you think you were doing?" he asked, the female shadow still at his side.

Olivia felt her throat get tight, and tears started running down her cheeks.

Brad laughed maniacally.

"Oh, you think your problems are so bad, little miss sweetheart, living in your deluded dreamland," Brad said with taunting rage. "What would you ever have to be sad about? Isn't your life perfect? Haven't you found your bliss?" He asked, mocking her.

She wiped the tears from her cheeks and looked at him while her own anger stoked inside.

"You wouldn't know the first thing about happiness," she said. "The only time you feel content is during those brief moments when you're off screwing your bitches . . ."

She looked at him, hoping to see the sting in his eyes, but he didn't falter.

"You have no idea who I am or why I do anything. Just because we're connected by this shadow shit doesn't mean I'm going to let you know jack about who I am."

Courtney returned from the back room, curious about the commotion going on. She approached Brad and touched his shoulder.

He turned to her and glared.

"Get out!" he bellowed and, like an old dog slapped too many times, Courtney skittered away without a word.

As soon as Courtney was gone, Olivia spoke.

"How could you sleep with someone like her?" she asked.

"Did Buzz tell you that I slept with Courtney? The ass. Well, I'll tell you why I did her. Because she's hot and easy. You, on the other hand, little lady, are not fuckable!"

Olivia pulled back, stung by his abrasive words.

"You know, I don't give a shit what you think of me, old man," Olivia said. "You're just some biker, probably infested with herpes and God know what else. You come off as all tough and calloused, but I know you. You're fucking afraid of your own shadow."

"Do you think the psychoanalytic ramblings of a spoiled girl who sells cupcakes for a living are going to faze me? You smug bitch!" Brad yelled.

Olivia clenched her fists. "You know, I'm glad I didn't waste my time screwing you. *Buzz* was a much better lay."

"What did you say?"

"Yeah, you heard right. In the cupcake shop. Right on the kitchen counter. It was amazing. He said I was like a 'cake-baking animal.' " She grinned like a self-satisfied cat. "He was a way better lay than you would ever be."

Laughter from both shadows filled the room.

"Congratulations," Brad said. "You've just banged the biggest prick in Saint Augustine. You should be proud of yourself, little miss cock hunter."

"You're just a soulless asshole who would rather stay in your cave than face the God damned world." She glared at him then spat on the floor in front of his feet. "Chicken shit," she said.

A network of lines embedded in Brad's face deepened, dark and devil-like, as he lunged forward. Wrapping his fingers around Olivia's throat, he held her tight.

She tried to yell, but with each protest he squeezed tighter, relishing her weak attempts to break free.

Olivia continued to struggle, twisting and turning, trying to wriggle her way out of his grasp, but he was too strong. She stabbed her nails into his hands, digging deep into the skin. Small drips of his blood trickled from her claws.

"Brad, please," she eked out as her throat tightened even more.

The shadows laughed again, only this time it was not just the voices of two disembodied creatures. Now another voice joined in—a third. This one was dark and low, and to Brad it was all too familiar. This was the laugh of a man with too much power—the sound his father made when he delighted in the pain of others.

This third voice was a tone so cruel, so familiar, it could have easily been mistaken for the voice of his mother's killer from many years ago, but Brad knew his father was long dead. The only madman in the room was him.

Brad looked at Olivia, her face turning purple in his hands, and he felt as if his own soul were seeping from his pores, a lifetime of pain being driven though his hands. Dizzy now, he released his grip, dropping the terrified woman to the floor. Olivia pulled back as far away as she could get from this monster.

Brad looked at the neon sign above her head. Buzzing in yellows and reds, the phoenix hung from its metal frame in a network of twisted glass tubes, reminding him who he really was. Not the killer, but a man who had seen too much, a man who was tired and broken but always returned whole. Brad looked from the sign down to the terrified woman who sat curled up on the floor.

With caution he approached Olivia, but she backed away, wedging herself into the corner.

The shadows' laughter began once again, but it seem stripped of its fervor. Brad was drawn back into his dream with Olivia.

He watched as her hand dipped with grace into the pond. This time, as she retrieved the glowing pearl, he knew she held the answer to the question he had never dared to ask. The answer had been there all along; he was simply too afraid to accept it. He reached out, and she placed the dripping wet sphere in his hand. In the moment he felt it—the corrosion of fear. He was here, in this space alive, straddling life's contradictions: dark and light, hot and cold, above and below, fear and joy. A perfect balance. Wholeness.

Brought back to the room, he looked to her broken, tired body.

"Oh Liv, I am sorry. I am so sorry," he said over and over again.

She watched from a safe distance away, the blinding pain of his hands around her neck still present in her mind. She was not ready to forgive.

Acutely aware of his aloneness, Brad placed his face in his hands and wept as a man whose truth had been revealed. As a solitary being, the tears continued, until he was nothing but the ashen remains of the man he had once been.

On his shoulders, he felt a gentle touch, two delicate, tentative arms wrapping around his body, a warm chest pressed against his back.

"Shh . . ." Olivia spoke softly into his ear. "It's okay."

Brad turned and looked at her.

"You're forgiven," she said. "I know it wasn't you."

"But it was, Liv. This shadow isn't new; it's the same darkness I've run from my whole life."

"Maybe so, but that piece of you is just that— a piece. It no longer rules you." And she pointed towards the center of the room where the ancient boxes rested.

In a dance of resignation, the shadows circled around each other in the double helix of life.

Brad smiled. He had spent his whole life denying himself, running from the devil within. He was worn out from a life of trying, and now he knew it was time to stop the fight.

He saw who he was—the darkness and the light. He no longer had anything to prove.

Brad turned to Olivia, brought his lips to her hand and kissed her cool skin, then together they watched the ballet of dark souls as they spun like wisps of dissipating smoke.

"It's beautiful," Olivia said.

He looked at her, her features illuminated almost golden in the light, and he saw the gift the shadows had given her. Freed from her bonds, she was now open to see the world not as a fearful girl but a fearless woman. This beautiful being was not a capricious wisp but something indelible and wise. He wanted her, not the quick lay, but the woman, the whole of her.

He brought her in close and ran his fingers through her fine hair then placed his lips on hers. She responded with softness, bringing her hand to the nape of his neck and pulling him in so close he could feel the power of her desire. They exhaled and inhaled together, their lips melting into one another, until neither was sure where the line stood between them.

Coaxed by their devils, applauded by their angels, Brad and Olivia fell into place. He brought his mouth to her throat and with passionate kisses followed it upward towards her ear. Her body arched. Feeling a wild ache so strong, it took all her strength to not consume him.

Brad's hands moved up the sides of her torso, clinging to her hips. Finding her breasts, he teased her nipples into arousal then traveled downward, his tongue toying with her navel for a moment, then wandering down to her inner thighs, where he moved like a panther to discover her darkness.

Olivia moaned as she felt herself bloom, rising in a cacophony of color, purples, pinks and reds. Life was nothing more than a layering of textures, swirls of passion, weaving itself within her. As she lay helpless, blissfully vulnerable, she felt Brad move in, and with a slow, dark glide he thrust forward, awakening her once again.

Her insides gripped tight as he moved within her. And, as he pushed into and out of this delicate being of water and light, he felt himself moved by a tribal rhythm, venturing in patterns known throughout time. In this perfect moment, he felt himself succumb. No longer part of his skin, he felt as if he split into a separate being, one that was moving infinitely outward.

There with Olivia, he felt as if he could reach out beyond the walls of the shop, beyond the trees, above the city, up to the stars, his only connection to the earth being her, the body of light he clung to.

The lovers collapsed, out of breath, sharing their ecstatic bliss in silence. As their heartbeats settled, Olivia turned and looked deeply at Brad's face, noting the river delta of lines at his eye, perfectly worn by time and tragedy. Although she had only known him for a few days, she felt she knew him wholly, that everything he was and ever would be was present within the blissful smile in his face.

Brad gave her a boyish grin. Olivia smiled back, feeling absolute satisfaction. Then, out of the stillness and the joy she began to giggle, her insides warm and completely at ease.

"Holy fuck, that was good," she said.

"Hell, yeah!" He laughed. "That was . . ." he paused.

"The best sex ever?" Olivia smiled.

"No, not really. I don't think that can even qualify as sex. That was like being shot from a cannon into another dimension."

Olivia watched with delight as his fingers traced the line of her breast.

"I think I saw God," she laughed.

"No shit. Me, too."

Just looking at his youthful smile made Olivia's belly feel warm.

She lifted herself onto one elbow.

"You are amazing, you know that?" she said.

"What can I say? It's a gift."

Olivia giggled. "Humility is clearly not one of your strong suits," she said. Staring at the stubble on his cheek, she began tracing the geography of his ear.

"Hey, being perfect isn't easy," he said, turning to kiss her on the cheek.

"No," she smiled, "I suppose not!" and she returned the kiss.

Brad turned his head to the shadows. Now, just a few feet high above the boxes, they spun in a spiral descent.

"You're not going to believe this," Brad said, "but I think they want in."

Olivia looked at them for a moment, stood and walked across the shop to where the boxes rested, her naked nymph-like body illuminated in oranges and reds from the neon sign. Poised to let them in, she paused.

"What if I'm not ready?" Olivia asked, biting her lip.

"How can you not be ready? After all this shit? Seriously?" Brad asked.

"I have spent my life in a box, Brad. Regardless of what bad things have come from the shadows, this opening has brought me freedom."

"I get that, but that doesn't mean we should have plans to go find more of them."

"Yeah, maybe. But this new me—this life—it's intoxicating."

"Yeah, but at what cost?"

"I know," Olivia frowned. "Being this open has made me hungry, both literally and figuratively. The more I get, the more I want. I feel like I could eat and eat and never be fulfilled—more chocolate, more sex, more adventure. It doesn't end."

"So, is that what you want for the rest of your life? To be haunted by shadows?"

"No, definitely not. I want to feel full, like I feel with you now, not that immediate need to be fulfilled, but something slow and safe."

He stood up and walked over to her and drew her in close to his body.

She looked up at him. "So, what do you think? When the shadows are gone, am I going to lose my power?"

"No, Dorothy, even without the ruby slippers, you've always had the power. It's in you!"

A small crease appeared between her eyes.

"Liv, everything the shadow gave you is still with you. I can see it in your eyes. You're not the bottled-up girl I met on Wednesday at the Bridge of Lions."

Olivia hugged him.

"Thank you," she said

"For what?"

"For showing me peace." She paused. "I'm ready now."

She looked at Brad, took a deep breath, and opened the lid of one of the boxes.

"*Non plus chaos.*" Olivia said aloud, and they watched as the male shadow was drawn into the box like a genie in reverse. Olivia closed the lid, latching the clasp. She brought the box to her heart, feeling it now warm against her chest.

"Your turn," she said as she turned to Brad.

He rose and brought the other box in his palm, then lifted the lid.

The two watched as the shadow danced like a music box ballerina in his hand. "So, long. *Non plus chaos,*" he said, and the female shadow swirled its way into the box. Brad slammed it shut.

"Good riddance," he said.

Olivia wrapped her arms around Brad and gave him a tight hug.

"Hold on, don't get too excited," Brad said "We're not done yet."

"What do you mean?" Olivia asked, exhausted.

"Come on, woman, we're going for a ride."

OPEN SOULS

Chapter 35

The light from Brad's headlight illuminated the park, lighting the Fairchild Oak from below. Brad killed the engine. He and Olivia hopped off the bike and approached the tree.

Even in the darkness of the night, the tree still felt welcoming, like a wise giant, its branches ascending into the infinite sky.

"So, you going to tell me what we're doing?" Olivia asked.

"We're leaving a box here."

"You sure? Shouldn't we take it back to the Lightner Museum?"

"So it can be stolen again by some other crazy cake-baker? No way." Brad smiled. "I thought we'd put it somewhere difficult to find."

Brad pulled himself up onto the low-lying limb and cautiously brought his feet forward, balancing on the old tree like he was a boy on a playground. Olivia, still on the ground, watched him climb higher and higher until he was just a faint smudge on a blackened canvas.

"That's got to be high enough," she called, her voice echoing through the trees.

"Just about," he called down, stopping at the spot where he and Olivia first kissed. Then, carefully positioning himself, he placed the box at a junction where two branches met. Before heading down, he paused and placed his hand on the great oak's trunk, letting himself feel the pulse of the tree. His thoughts went to Dog, but he felt no sadness, instead he felt a stirring of joy. His friend had led a good life. Dog had lived hard, but he did everything with passion and love. Brad smiled and headed down to where Olivia stood waiting.

After an hour's ride back to Saint Augustine, they crossed the Bridge of Lions. Brad pulled to the side of the road, and they both climbed off.

Olivia watched as Brad walked with the box over to the eastern-most lion.

"I'm doing this one," she said, catching up to him and taking the box. She pulled herself up and placed the box back beside the lion's foot, then patted the statue's rock solid mane and smiled.

"Where to, now?" she asked Brad.

"One more spot, not too far away," he said. "I've got something to finish."

Brad climbed on the bike.

"Where?" she asked.

"You know where, woman. It's time. You're getting that tattoo," he said, "only now it's all you, no shadow breathing down your neck. You still want to do it?"

"Absolutely!" She smiled as she climbed on the bike.

As Brad pulled away, he paused to look one more time at the lion, when he noticed something hovering above the statue. A silvery osprey was soaring just a few feet overhead, its feathered silhouette a beacon in the black of the night.

"Liv! Look." he said as he pointed upward.

Her eyes lit up.

"It's her," she said.

The bird circled over their heads, appearing to hold them in her sight.

"Thank you," Olivia called out to the bird.

The bird shook its wings, and a tiny feather fell from its body. Olivia's eye followed the feather's path as it came to land just a few feet from them. She jumped off the bike, picked it up and let it lightly touch her cheek.

"We're free," Olivia said as she climbed back on the bike and wrapped her arms around Brad.

He smiled, his focus still on the bird as it headed out to sea and said, "Yes, we are."

www.OpenSoulsBook.com

A Note from the Author-

While writing this story, I found myself listening to songs that brought life to what I was writing in the book. Below are some of the songs I listened to as I wrote, as well as the ones mentioned in the book.

Sympathy for the Devil, by the Rolling Stones, seemed appropriate. Although I never thought of the shadows as agents of the Devil, they sure seemed to wreak havoc on people's lives.

Shadow on the Run, by Black Rebel Motorcycle Club, felt like a perfect companion to Brad's tired mind.

I chose *I Can't Get No Satisfaction*, by the Stones, with poor Olivia in mind, whose endless longings couldn't be fulfilled. In the end she gets—maybe not all that she wants—but at least she gets what she needs.

I first heard Jimmy Page's and Robert Plant's live version of **Kashmir** on the *No Quarter* album with my husband one late night while we were just hanging out, listening to music. This version is recorded with the Egyptian Orchestra, which provides a slow, seductive Middle Eastern feel. It seemed like the perfect music to offer Olivia as she danced her way into ecstasy.

OPEN SOULS

I heard **10,000 Angels**, by Edie Brickell & New Bohemians, the other day while driving in my car down the stretch of ocean highway that Brad and Olivia rode their motorcycle along. This song was a favorite back when I was in college and seemed appropriate for the book as it personifies the pull between control and chaos.

Whirling, the album by Omar Faruk Tekbilek, is one of my favorites. I listened to Mr. Tekbilek on Pandora while I wrote, enjoying the mix of Turkish music that Pandora offered. Listening to Tekbilek was perfect when crafting the final sex scene!

Om Namaha Shivaya, by Robert Gass and On Wings of Song, is a version of an ancient chant that I have listened to for most of my adult life. I often sing it to my children at bedtime as it has an amazing calming effect. There's something sad yet also joyous about this simple mantra, making it the perfect song for Brad as he puts his pain to rest.

Acknowledgments

First, I want to thank friend and fellow author **Tim Baker,** whose honesty and support have been paramount to this project. This book is better because of him. Tim also came up with the title. Thank you Tim!

Then, of course, **Shawn Pourchot**, my wonderful, tolerant husband who has listened to me process this book every frickin' step of the way. He let me bounce ideas off him, gave me some of his own, and tolerated the random moments when I'd run to grab paper, saying, "Hold on! I've got an idea!"

Much thanks to editor **Karin Nicely**, whose quick and diligent editing skills have helped make this a book to be proud of.

Thank you to **Petra Iston** for the beautiful cover design. Aside from being a great painter, she is a wonderful graphic artist. I gave her my ideas and she came back quickly with her smoky impressions of my book.

Thank you to friends **Camica Bennett**, **Brandi Jagger**, and **John Pascucci** for being my initial beta read team. The book has come a long way since my first attempt, and I was grateful for their wonderful scrutinizing attention to detail. And thank you to **Yasmine Oshri** and **Mary Rogers-Grantham** for doing the final read through.

Then many thanks to my second run of beta readers (or should I say gamma readers?) **Karisa Johnson**, **Abby Schumwinger**, and **Nichole Fromm**. I knew I could count on them to be critical and thoughtful in their reviews. Thank you, gals!

Over the course of writing this book, I got two tattoos, and naturally that affected the fate of this book. My tattoo artist, **Donny Brey**, is good at what he does. Really good. During my second tattoo, I grilled him on all the details and inner workings of his shop. I hope I got it right, Donny.

David Karner helped me work through ideas for a screenplay for this book, but more importantly, he is a fabulous cheerleader (pom poms not included). He never doubts my passion . . . or anyone else's for that matter. David is a good all-around guy, and I'm happy to have him around.

Suzanne Stewart and **Craig Harris** of **Change Jar Books** have supported me since my very first book was just an idea. They have been a constant source of support over the years and pour their love into everything they do. Thank you!

Made in the USA
Columbia, SC
27 November 2021